From the day Abby was born, no woman could catch his imagination

The practice and his role of bachelor father had kept Jon fully occupied—until now. Amazingly, Laura was back in his life. He couldn't help but remember all they'd said and done together. How they'd laughed at the same jokes, liked the same things, looked forward to roaming the fields together and playing down by the river, and how they'd then moved into adolescence together. It had all been so uncomplicated, until they'd gone to university....

The yearning to see the old Laura back again consumed him. The Laura with hair as gold as the corn at harvest time. The Laura who'd saved all her smiles for *him*.

Dear Reader,

If we have met before, welcome, and if we haven't, hello.

We are back in the beautiful English countryside again, and love is in bloom for Laura and Jon. I do hope that you will enjoy sharing in their heartaches and misunderstandings until they find that magical thing called romance.

Very best regards,

Abigail

A SINGLE DAD AT HEATHERMERE
Abigail Gordon

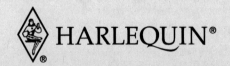

TORONTO • NEW YORK • LONDON
AMSTERDAM • PARIS • SYDNEY • HAMBURG
STOCKHOLM • ATHENS • TOKYO • MILAN • MADRID
PRAGUE • WARSAW • BUDAPEST • AUCKLAND

ISBN-13: 978-0-373-06636-0
ISBN-10:   0-373-06636-8

A SINGLE DAD AT HEATHERMERE

First North American Publication 2008

A SINGLE DAD AT HEATHERMERE

CHAPTER ONE

DRIVING home from the airport, Jon Emmerson had no idea that the past was about to catch up with him. He and Abby had spent the last three weeks with his sister and her family in Australia and now, invigorated and relaxed, he was about to once more take up the reins of the country practice where he was senior partner.

As his glance rested on his eight-year-old daughter sitting beside him, Jon was remembering the pleasure of watching her get to know her cousins in a far-away country. He wished that Abby wasn't an only child, but he was a man who took his responsibilities seriously.

Bringing her up on his own, at the same time as being in charge of the medical practice in Heathermere, the village where he'd been brought up, left little time for becoming involved in new relationships, and if he did have the time he would have to have the taste for them first.

As he drove through the leafy lanes of Cheshire, the pleasure of coming home increased. His mother would be waiting to greet them, bursting to know all there was to know about her daughter, son-in-law, and their children in Australia, and ready with a big hug for the granddaughter that she usually saw every day.

They had reached the village and as they drove past the back garden of elderly Harry Hewitt's house, Jon's attention was caught by a small, fair-haired boy kicking a ball about there. Washing hung from the clothesline, but instead of Harry's sensible smalls wafting in the breeze, there were boys' shorts and T-shirts, and women's wear.

Abby was delighted to see her beloved grandmother, and after a delicious lunch was soon rediscovering her toys. Jon had given his mother all his news and, as they sat enjoying a cup of tea, he asked about the little boy he'd seen earlier in the village. 'What's going on at Harry's place, Mum? There was a child playing in his garden,' he asked.

In her late sixties, with hair still as dark and glossy as her son's, Marjorie Emmerson had two great loves in her life—her family, and the village where she lived. But the pleasure of having her son and granddaughter back home was diminishing with his question.

'We've had a funeral in the village while you've been gone,' she replied.

'Not Harry!'

'I'm afraid so.'

'How? When?' he asked.

'The day after you flew out. He fell off the roof of the outhouse and was badly injured. I took the liberty of rummaging through his desk and found Laura's contact details. When I phoned her she came straight away. He never recovered, but she was able to spend some time with him after so many years apart, and I feel that maybe some sort of a reconciliation followed before he died. Harry had been a poor sort of father and as the years have gone by we both know that he'd almost become a recluse.

'He never got over losing her mother when Laura was only small and always saw her as an encumbrance rather than a comfort. But you already know that, don't you? It was why Laura was always round at our place. The little one you saw in the garden would be her son, Liam.'

'So she has a child.'

'Yes. He's five years old.'

'I see, and so where was she living when you phoned her?'

'Cornwall.' Marjorie sighed. 'She's changed, Jon. If I hadn't known she was coming, I wouldn't have recognised her.'

'Haven't we all,' he said wryly. 'And what about Freddie? Is he with her?'

Marjorie shook her head. 'No. There's been no mention of him. Maybe he couldn't get away.'

Jon frowned as he thought about the girl who had been his childhood friend. He and Laura had been brought up together in the rural paradise that was still his home. They'd both decided to go into medicine and had been accepted by the same university, but they'd soon drifted apart.

He had taken to their new life like a duck to water. In the excitement of studying for what had always been his chosen career he had become involved with different friends and different agendas as his dark good looks and outgoing personality had drawn others to him.

Whenever he thought back to those days he was reminded of how he'd left Laura to find her own niche. Being of a quieter nature than him, it had taken her some time, and he was ashamed that he'd been so selfish. Instead of being there for his friend, he'd been too engrossed in his own affairs.

She'd settled in eventually and they'd been pleasant enough to each other when they met back home on vacations, but he'd always had somewhere that he'd been dashing off to, and gradually she'd retreated into the background of his life and had found friends of her own. Then she'd gone on to marry Freddie, moving out of the area and out of Jon's life once and for all.

As she watched her son romping around the garden that had been her own childhood escape place, Laura's mind was made up. She was going back to Cornwall at the first opportunity. Her father's house was rented until the end of the month, which gave her a couple of weeks to sort out his affairs and then someone else would be moving in. They'd already paid the deposit, and in any case the last thing she wanted was to live there.

All her happy childhood memories were of the time she'd spent with the Emmersons, and Jon in particular. She'd discovered since coming back to the village for her father's funeral that he had never married and had been amazed that in the eight years since he'd broken up with Kezia Carter he hadn't met anyone else. She'd also found out that he was in charge of the medical practice…and that his mother helped to look after the child that had put an end to her own hopes and dreams.

It was odd that they were each bringing up a child on their own. It had a feeling of affinity about it. Yet any closeness they'd had was long gone. When she'd discovered that Jon and his daughter had been on holiday in Australia she'd felt relieved.

Coming back to Heathermere had brought back a lot of old memories, and a few times she'd felt the urge to stay. Marjorie Emmerson had been kind and supportive all the time she'd been coping with her father's accident and his subsequent death, and so had other people. But the person who had been most in her thoughts since she'd come back had been Jon, who had been far away and known nothing of what had been going on in his absence.

It was better that she return to Cornwall before he came home. That way they would avoid the embarrassment of meeting again as strangers.

It was a warm summer night. Liam was fast asleep, tucked up in the bed that used to be hers, and as Laura stood in the open kitchen doorway, looking out aimlessly, she saw him coming. Striding towards her across the field at the back of the house. He was home, she thought. She hadn't been quick enough in her intention to return to where she'd come from.

The face that she hadn't seen for many a long year was set in sombre lines, so Marjorie must have told him about her father, she thought, and he had come to offer his condolences.

'Laura,' he said quietly when he came to a halt in front

of her. 'It's been a long time.' She was hoping there might be regret in his voice, but there was only flat politeness as he went on to say, 'I'm sorry to hear about your father. My mother told me what had happened when I arrived back from Australia just a few hours ago.'

'Yes. It was very sudden,' she told him stiffly.

'Is there anything I can do?'

She was taking in every detail of him. It had been over eight years since she'd last looked on the dark appeal of him, and with a glint of silver in his hair and a few lines beneath the hazel eyes fixed on hers, he was still something to look at.

And what was *she*? Too thin. Salt-blown and sun-bleached, with fashion a word that women with money to throw around used.

She stepped back to let him in, thinking that this unexpected meeting would be best conducted inside, but he shook his head.

'No, thanks. I'm due back at the surgery tomorrow and haven't unpacked yet. I just felt that I must have a quick word.' He looked around him. 'Isn't Freddie with you?'

She shook her head. 'Freddie was drowned shortly after Liam was born. He was caught in a fast current while we were having a beach picnic in Cornwall.'

He was staring at her, aghast. 'That is dreadful! I had no idea! You were left to bring up your son on your own?'

She nodded stiffly. 'Yes. I still live in Cornwall, in the same house, and work part time at the local surgery.'

'So we're both GPs.'

'Mmm. I guess so.' She managed a faint smile. 'Though I never imagined you ending up here.'

Jon shrugged. 'Circumstances alter cases. I had a child to bring up. I decided that village life with a loving grandma in the background would give her a better chance than crèches and childminders in a city environment. She's called Abby. She's eight years old, and she lights up my life.'

Laura nodded, hearing the love in his voice. 'And what about Kezia?'

'Gone.' His tone instantly changed. 'Haven't heard anything of her since she made a quick getaway after Abby's birth. She gave me full custody. Anything to shed the responsibility.'

'I see.'

'Well, that's enough of the past. What about the future, Laura? If you decide to sell this place, it will soon go and you'll get plenty for it. Properties in the Cheshire countryside are in big demand.'

'I won't be doing that. You've probably forgotten that this is a rented cottage,' she told him woodenly, and wished she could turn the clock back to the days when they'd shared every thought with each other.

He frowned. 'Yes, of course. I *had* forgotten. So what are you going to do? Go back to Cornwall?'

'I haven't decided. Everything happened so suddenly,' she told him in the same flat tone, but she knew that wasn't true. Her mind had been made up until he'd come striding back into her life a few moments ago.

'Yes, I can understand that,' he said gravely, and as he turned to go, he added, 'Can I just say that if there is anything I can do to make this sad time in your life any easier, you have only to ask.'

'Thank you.' She nodded coolly and watched him depart, tall, straight-backed and nothing like the impetuous medical student who'd fallen for another student and had found out that she didn't want to be tied down by a child.

Laura had looked pale and low in spirits, Jon thought as he walked back to his mother's house, and it wasn't surprising if she'd just laid her father to rest in the graveyard beside the village church. Not to mention losing her husband in such a tragic way.

He'd been dumbstruck when she'd told him about Freddie. It seemed that after all this time they still had something in common. They were both single parents, as poor Freddie hadn't been around for long after they'd got married.

It was weird that Laura had never come back to the place where she had been born. He regretted the years of non-communication and it was his fault. He'd had his first taste of freedom and had pushed her to one side, treating all that they'd been to each other when they'd been young as nothing compared to the excitement of college life.

He'd been amazed when she'd married Freddie Cavendish, another medical student, shortly after they'd all qualified. Steady Freddie, he'd called him when she'd told him her news, reliable, agreeable and...

She'd flared up at that and said, 'How about minding your own business? I don't interfere in your life.'

There had been times since when he'd wished she had. But at least there had been blessings from their respective relationships. Blessings in abundance, in the form of a small dark-haired girl who held his heart, and the sturdy, golden-haired boy he'd seen kicking a ball around in old Harry's garden.

Kezia had become pregnant in his last term at college, and their relationship had foundered. She'd made no bones about telling him she didn't want that kind of responsibility. When she'd talked about a termination their passion had soured.

He'd been feeling miserable and guilty and had insisted that it was his child, too. He'd wanted it and had told her he would bring it up alone if she felt so strongly. It seemed that she did. Abby's arrival hadn't caused her to change her mind. So he'd taken over. Gone as a locum at the village surgery and with his mother's help had begun to care for the tiny person who had turned his life around.

There had been times when money had been short and he had been exhausted, but he had no regrets. Whenever he looked at Abby he knew he'd made the right decision.

Had Laura made the right decision about marrying Freddie? he wondered. It sounded as if she hadn't had much time to find out. It was awful what had happened to the poor guy.

Only now had he discovered her situation. Had her father known? he wondered, but decided that he couldn't have done. Surely Harry would have said something. Yet he and Laura had never been close. She'd had a miserable childhood.

He wanted to go back and explain that what he'd said about selling the house had been merely something to say. There had been no hidden meaning in it, but it had sounded as if he didn't want her to stay. She may have looked dejected, he thought, but Laura had a mind of her own. He hadn't always got his own way when they'd been young, and she would take a dim view of him telling her what to do now.

'That is terrible!' his mother exclaimed when Jon told her about Freddie. 'Some of us wondered where he was at such a time, but we didn't like to pry, and Laura never explained his absence. She should have come back home to be with the people who knew and loved her when she lost her husband.'

'Obviously she didn't want to,' he remarked dryly. 'But the past is past and a certain young lady should be going home to bed. Where is she?'

His mother smiled. 'Still playing.'

'So I'll go and have a cuddle and then I'll take her home,' he said, anxious to get back to normality after those uncomfortable moments on the back doorstep of Harry Hewitt's house, and as he and Abby laughed and played Jon began to relax.

But he wasn't relaxed during the midnight hours when Abby was asleep in the apartment above the surgery where they lived. In recent years he'd achieved a degree of contentment in his life. The practice meant a lot to him, but even more than that his daughter was the centre of his existence, and he had a great love for his mother who so often put her affairs on hold for their sakes.

He'd had no taste for relationships since he'd last seen Laura. He'd made one mistake with Kezia and was not going to make another. But seeing Laura again had shaken him. She'd been part of the fabric of his life before he'd stepped onto shifting sands, and he could kick himself for waffling on about house prices like some pushy estate agent. But she'd soon reminded him that the house wasn't hers to sell.

He would like to see her back where she belonged. Not for his sake, but for hers and her son's. She was a GP and he and Tim Gosforth, his junior partner, had room for a part-time doctor to help with their steadily growing list of patients.

Jon had intended specialising in paediatrics when he'd got his degree, but with a child to care for he'd gone into general practice on his own patch to give Abby a stable home life. He'd worked first as a locum, then as junior partner in the village practice. Now he was in charge, and he wondered what she would say if he offered her a position there. She'd looked so drained and stressed out, it was the least he could do if she intended staying.

When Jon had gone Laura stood like someone mesmerised. Their reunion, if it warranted such a description, had been unsettling and upsetting. If she'd known he was coming she might have achieved some degree of composure, but as it was she'd been stunned to see him.

When she'd calmed down she went slowly upstairs and stood looking down at Liam. If she came back, where would they live? The cottage in Cornwall would bring a reasonable amount, but she would have to sell it before she could look for somewhere here, and, as Jon had explained, prices in the Cheshire countryside would be a lot higher than she would get for the home she'd shared with Freddie.

Her father had left her a little money, but it would be like a drop in the ocean if she bought a property in the village, and the question would be where and how.

You've soon changed your mind, she told herself. One glimpse of Jon and you're prepared to throw caution to the winds. Maybe a chat with the local estate agent will help to clear your head. It was sensible thinking. But did any of that matter? In the last hour an old friendship had taken a feeble step towards a new beginning.

The following evening, as Liam played in the garden before bedtime, Laura sat deep in thought on an old bench that had been there ever since she could remember.

The estate agent she'd spoken to that morning had echoed what Jon had said almost word for word, but it hadn't affected her new resolve. Cornwall was a beautiful place to live, but ever since Freddie had died it had lost its appeal, and her heart had always been in Heathermere, where she had been born. It would be a fresh start, and she knew the village would be a wonderful place for her son to grow up.

Laura needed a quick sale of the cottage in Cornwall and then she would be able to balance her budget. She knew that any property she could afford would be very basic, but the urge to come back to live in Heathermere was becoming stronger by the minute. She kept pushing to one side the thought that she'd been going to do the exact opposite until she'd seen Jon again.

Something more important than money was affect-
ing her judgement.

They'd both changed out of all recognition, but they
would be living in the same community once more, and
even if they never became close again, it would be better
than nothing, as, apart from Liam, nothing was what
she'd had for a long time.

She looked at her young son playing happily with his
toy truck. He would have been starting school in Cornwall
in two weeks' time. So by enrolling him at the one in the
village she wouldn't be uprooting him from somewhere
that he'd only just settled into. It was the same one that
she'd gone to herself, a single-storey, sprawling building
of local limestone, just off the main street.

She and Jon had both gone there when they'd been
small and, no doubt, his daughter would be doing the
same. The thought of their children being at the same
school would need some adjusting to, and she hoped he
wouldn't see it as an intrusion into the life he'd made
for himself.

She was moving on too fast, she told herself. There
was still the small matter of finance. If she didn't get a
buyer for the cottage, she wouldn't be moving back, and
the thought of that filled her with gloom.

The following day, Jon called again in the middle of his
house calls and Laura greeted him warily. She had
bumped into Marjorie down at the shops that morning
and during their friendly chat, let slip that she was
thinking of staying. She knew that Marjorie would have
told Jon of their conversation and wasn't sure how he

would react, whether he would be pleased, sorry or just not interested.

'I believe you're staying,' he said.

'Yes. If I can get a buyer for my cottage,' she told him, without meeting his glance. 'Then I will look for something small here.'

'Well, when you're ready there is a part-time job at the practice available if you're interested. We could fix the hours to fit in with your son's school times.'

Her eyes widened in surprise. 'What would I be doing?' she asked carefully, knowing from what she'd heard people say that there were already two doctors there. Maybe they wanted someone to keep the place clean and make the tea.

Jon stared at her with surprised dark eyes. 'You would be working there as an extra GP. What else? You told me that's what you've been doing in Cornwall.'

She nodded, stunned by this unexpected turn of events. 'Yes, it is.'

'So think about it, Laura. There's no rush. Sort out your affairs and then let me know what you've decided. I've been thinking we need extra help for a while and it could solve both of our problems. That is, if you need employment.'

'Oh, I will need it all right,' she assured him. 'Properties here are twice the price of houses in Cornwall, and Liam and I have to live. But are you sure that you would want me on your staff?'

'Why not? It will depend on how capable a doctor you are, and if I remember rightly, we both got good degrees, even though in my case I'd made a hash of everything else.'

'The head of the practice in Cornwall would give me a reference and the primary care trust would soon let you know if I have any black marks against me,' she pointed out, ignoring his last comment.

She could imagine elderly James Penrose's expression when he discovered she was leaving the Cornwall practice. The grizzled Cornishman who was senior partner there was a good friend. He'd been kind and supportive and Liam saw him as a grandfatherly figure.

But James would always want what was best for them both and would be pleased to know that she was sorting her life out in the place where she'd grown up.

'Why are you doing this?' she asked, not wanting to leave the matter there. 'You don't owe me anything, Jon.'

'I know that. I am offering you the job because it is what I would do for anyone that I thought might be suitable. Now I must go. I have calls to do and in our family we try to have our evening meal together. It gives me the chance to hear what Abby and my mother have been doing with their day, and after we've eaten Abby and I have our special time until she goes to bed.'

'It must have been a relief to have had your mother around since Abby was born,' she commented.

He nodded. 'Mum is a gem. It would have been very difficult without her.'

He looked at her, his dark eyes serious. 'You haven't had any family to support you, have you? But now you're staying there'll be lots of people here who've never forgotten you and will want to help.'

'Hmm. Maybe,' she said coolly. 'But I am used to coping.'

'Yes, I'm sure you are,' he said dryly. 'Otherwise you might have let some of us know that you were bringing up your child on your own.' And on that note of censure he went.

Jon didn't have to patronise her, she thought as he disappeared from view. Had he expected her to come running back home when her life had fallen apart with Freddie's death? She wouldn't have come back, no matter what. Her father would have had scant comfort to offer, and she and Jon had become too estranged.

He'd made it clear that the offer of the job at the practice wasn't personal so there was no point in reading anything into it, but it had come as a surprise and a welcome one at that. It would mean that she wouldn't be far away from Liam when he was at school, and she'd seen that during the holidays there was a play-group that met there for children whose parents were working. She would manage somehow.

Now she was eager for the sale of her property to go through with all speed. She was being given the chance to come back to Heathermere and begin a new life with Liam. For the first time in ages she felt happy and relaxed, even though she didn't know where they were going to live.

Her son came in from the garden at that moment and when she opened her arms wide he ran into them and looked up at her with his bright blue gaze.

'Who was that man, Mummy?' he asked. 'He said, "Hello, Liam".'

'His name is Jon Emmerson,' she told him as she planted a kiss on his smooth cheek. 'He is a doctor, like me. We used to play together when I was only as big as you. He wants me to work at the surgery with him, like I've been doing with Dr Penrose in Cornwall.'

'And are you going to?'

'Yes, I think so. You know that Heathermere is where I was born, don't you? That I went to the school just down the road?'

He nodded his small golden head and wanted to know, 'So are we going to live here and will I be going to that school?'

'Yes. Do you think you will like that?'

'Mmm, I will,' he told her cheerfully, 'but we don't have to stay in Grandad's house, do we?'

'No, my little love, we don't,' she told him, and thought, not even if they had to live in a tent.

CHAPTER TWO

THE following day Laura phoned James Penrose at the surgery in Cornwall and told him of her plans. His reaction was what she'd expected. The elderly Cornishman was sad to see her go, but happy for her and Liam to be starting a new life among old friends and acquaintances.

'Now I've made the decision I'm anxious to get my affairs sorted. I need to sell my cottage as soon as possible,' she told him, 'but as summer is almost over I can't see a big demand for holiday homes or small properties at the moment.'

She heard him chuckle at the other end of the line. 'You could be wrong there, lassie. I'll buy it off you… furnished, if you like.'

'You, James!' she exclaimed. 'It's only a quarter of the size of your house.'

'Yes, I know. But the situation is this. Millie and I are getting a bit old for having our children and their children staying with us for weeks on end in the summer. We love having them but it can be a bit much. I've been on the lookout for a cottage like yours where they can stay separate from us and yet be near.

So you have a buyer, my dear.'

'That's wonderful,' she choked. 'I can't believe it. You aren't doing this because you're sorry for me, are you?'

'No. Of course not. I'm fond of you, Laura, and want to see you happy. If moving back to this village of yours will bring that about I'll be only too pleased. Let me know the name and address of the solicitor you're going to use and I'll get in touch.'

When they'd finished their conversation Laura sank down onto the nearest chair and tried to take it in. James was going to buy her cottage. The die was cast. Some unseen force was shaping the future. She would be able to tell Jon that she would take the position he'd offered and set the wheels turning to find Liam a place in the village school.

She hoped Jon wouldn't have changed his mind about her working at the practice. The feeling that the offer had been made on impulse kept coming over her and that now maybe he was regretting it. If that was the case she would rather tell him face to face that she was definitely staying in the village and would be happy to be involved in the practice. That way she would be able to tell if he'd been having second thoughts.

That evening she went to the big stone house where she had played with Jon as a child. In those days his father had been alive, but his mother still lived there from all accounts and she was presuming that he and his daughter lived there, too.

With Liam gazing around curiously beside her, she rang the bell. There was no answer. About to retrace her steps, Laura was brought to a halt by the sound of voices. Seconds later Jon and a small girl who had her father and grandmother's dark good looks came round from the back of the house and stopped in surprise when they saw her and Liam on the doorstep.

'Hi,' he said easily, as if her calling round was nothing out of the ordinary. 'I thought I heard the bell. How long have you been here? My mother has gone to a meeting in the village hall and Abby and I were playing tennis on the back lawn.'

His glance was resting on Liam, who was smiling across at a solemn-faced Abby, and he said in greeting, 'Hello, there, Liam.' Then he turned to Laura. 'He reminds me of you when we sat next to each other on our first day at primary school. Except that you had your hair in plaits, if you remember.'

Of course she remembered. She remembered everything they'd ever said and done, but most of all she remembered how she'd adored him, had had a secret crush on him at the time they'd gone to university and had thought that once they were out in the wide, wide world they would be drawn together by their affection for each other.

The dream had been short-lived, and as their college days had gone by, Jon's affair with Kezia Carter in the last year of their course had finally set the seal on the separate lives they'd been living ever since going to university.

When he'd reluctantly told her that Kezia was pregnant with his baby she'd been devastated. But it had finally made her realise that they had no future together, and with the news that Kezia didn't want the baby and that he was going to become a single father to his child, she had realised even more that there was no place for her in his life, short of taking on the role of a secondhand rose.

Marrying Freddie some time later had been like stepping into calm waters after a ride on a rough sea. They'd had a loving marriage that she had expected to last forever, but it wasn't to be and it had become her turn to be a single parent, but for a very different reason.

Abby of the beautiful dark hair and eyes was fidgeting, wanting to get back to what they'd been doing, and it was clear that she was wondering who these strange people were.

'Yes, I do remember,' she told him in a low voice. Flashing Abby a friendly smile, she said, 'We've interrupted your game, haven't we, Abby? I won't keep your father long.' She turned to Jon. 'I'm here to tell you that I've sold my house. When I rang the surgery in Cornwall the senior partner there said he would like to buy it for when his family come to stay. So I can accept your job offer, if it is still open.'

'Yes. It's still open,' he said, his expression giving nothing away. 'When can you start?'

'Next week if they can take Liam into the school, and in the meantime I will have to find some temporary accommodation until my finances are sorted.'

'I don't see you having any problem with the school,' he said. 'And how would you fancy living over the surgery? There are two apartments up there. Abby and I live in one and the other is to let furnished.'

'Are you sure?' she said slowly, with the feeling that some unseen force really was at work in her life.

'I'm sure that there is a vacant apartment there, yes,' he said dryly, his eyes glinting with amusement.

'You know what I meant. Are you sure that you would want us in such close proximity?'

He was laughing and Laura thought it was the first time she'd seen him anything other than sombre since they'd renewed their aquaintance.

'Why? Have you got something catching?' he teased and she smiled.

'No. I'm just amazed at what you're suggesting. It's as if you have a magic wand that solves all my problems. I would be grateful to rent the apartment and thanks for the offer.'

'Why not call in at the practice the first chance you get so that you can view the accommodation and meet the staff? I have a junior partner called Tim Gosforth, who will be keen to introduce himself, and the rest of those working there are mostly local people. You might even know some of them.

'What about Liam after school? Have you thought about that?' he asked.

He glanced at the smiling child beside her again before switching back to Abby, and the thought flashed through his mind that anyone who didn't know the children might take the four of them for a family, so strong were their resemblances to their respective parents.

'There is a playgroup available for after school hours and holidays. So I will have to use that, I'm afraid,' she replied, and wondered where his thoughts had moved on to. From his expression he wasn't tuned in to what she was saying and for a moment he gazed at her blankly.

'What? Oh, yes. It's a facility for working parents, but I did promise we would try to arrange your hours to suit school times. I would be having the same kind of problem myself if my mother wasn't around.'

"I'm thirsty, Daddy,' Abby said, tired of waiting. 'Can I go to get a drink?'

'Yes, sure. Take Liam with you and get him one.'

When they'd disappeared round the side of the house, with Liam skipping along happily and Abby not sure whether she wanted this strange boy tagging along, Jon said, 'Aren't you going to come inside for a moment? We don't usually keep visitors standing on the doorstep.'

His tone was polite but not effusive and Laura could feel her colour rising. He was making it clear that was what he saw her as. A visitor to be treated with the casual courtesy he would offer to any caller.

From her own point of view she felt as if she was more of a reminder of a time he would like to forget than a visitor. But circumstances had brought her back into his life again and with no strings attached he was trying to be helpful. She supposed she ought to be grateful for that.

She managed a smile. 'I will come in for a moment, thank you, but mustn't stay long. It is almost Liam's bedtime.'

He was opening the door and standing back for her to pass him, and for a second they were close enough for Laura to feel the warmth of him against her. Then they were inside. She could hear the children's voices in the kitchen somewhere and Jon was asking, 'What about you, Laura? What can I get you to drink? A sherry? Tea? Coffee?'

'Er...a coffee would be nice, thank you.'

As he disappeared into the kitchen Abby and Liam came out sucking on ice lollies and Laura had to smile as she thought that perhaps Abby had decided that they were the quickest way to get Liam back to where he belonged, so that she and her father could carry on with their game of tennis.

When Jon came back with the coffee she said impulsively, 'I don't want to make a nuisance of myself, Jon. I can see that you have your life mapped out and we don't owe each other anything, do we?'

He was frowning. 'No. I don't suppose we do. But I feel that you've had it rough over recent years. For the sake of old times I'm doing what I can to help, and once again can I say feel free to ask if there is anything else that I can do for you.'

I won't be doing that, she wanted to tell him. He'd already found her a job and somewhere to live, freeing her from worry on both matters, but she hadn't come back as a charity case.

They didn't stay long. It was Liam's bedtime as she'd said, but their departure was more because being with Jon in a domestic setting wasn't easy to cope with. There was an atmosphere of relaxed living in his mother's attractive house that would make returning to the gloomy property that had been her father's even less welcoming.

As they walked the short distance between the two

houses, Laura told herself that soon they would be out of there. A new future was opening out before them and it was all due to the man who had once held her heart in uncaring hands and was now making amends, quite unaware of how much he still meant to her.

Freddie had known that she'd once had a crush on Jon. When he'd asked her to marry him she'd told him that Jon was in the past and had meant it, and their marriage had been good. For one thing Liam had been born of it, but sadly Freddie hadn't lived to see him grow up and there would always be sadness in her when she thought about that.

When Liam was asleep she went upstairs and stood looking through the bedroom window. The village green wasn't far away. She could see fat ducks waddling beside a pool where waterlilies floated, and there was a heron standing unmoving beside a young willow tree.

Beyond it she could see the roof of the house that she'd visited earlier among the trees, and thinking back to those moments with Jon, it had seemed as if he was living a contented bachelor sort of life with Abby.

It was incredible that he hadn't found someone else while she'd been gone. Had he had any relationships since his affair with Kezia had foundered? she wondered. It would be surprising if he hadn't. He had the looks, the job—*and* a ready-made family, which could create a problem for some, she supposed.

But with a lifting of her spirits she thought that life was going to be good from now on. Working beside him, doing the job she loved and watching Liam grow up in the place where she'd spent her own young life would be joys she hadn't expected to find when she'd come back because of her father's accident.

There wasn't any problem getting Liam accepted into the school and sorting out his uniform, and once that was done she did as Jon had suggested and called in at the surgery to view the apartment and meet the staff.

They hadn't been in contact since the night she'd gone to tell him that she was staying. She'd seen him driving around the village on his house calls and he'd smiled, waved at her briefly and gone on his way.

She visited the surgery in the middle of the afternoon, knowing from experience that it was usually a quiet time, and found it to be so. There were a few patients in the waiting room, booked in for the later surgery of the day, but it would be nothing like the morning's surgery.

A middle-aged receptionist behind the desk smiled when she saw Liam looking longingly at the children's corner and asked, 'Can I help you?'

Laura nodded. It felt good to be back on surgery premises, if only briefly.

'My name is Laura Cavendish,' she told her. 'I'm going to be joining the practice soon as a part-time doctor. Jon Emmerson suggested that I come in and introduce myself.'

The woman's smile deepened. 'Really? This is a surprise.' She held out a neatly manicured hand. 'I'm Denise Dobson. There are three of us in Reception and we do part-time hours, too. Then there are the practice nurses, Kathy and Melanie. Alison Arkwright is the practice manager, and Tim Gosforth, the junior partner.'

'Did I hear my name mentioned?' a voice asked from behind as the door swung open and when Laura turned a youngish man with a shock of russet hair was looking at them enquiringly.

'I'm here to introduce myself,' Laura said again. 'I'm joining the practice on a part-time basis.'

'Ah, you must be Laura,' he said. 'Jon mentioned you only this morning.'

He flashed her a friendly smile. 'It will be good to have you with us. I'm Tim Gosforth, as you will have guessed.'

'Laura Cavendish,' she informed him as they shook hands. 'I've just moved back into the village. I needed employment and Jon offered me the position.'

While they'd been speaking Liam had let go of his mother's hand and was happily amusing himself on a wooden rocking horse.

'Is the youngster yours?' Tim asked.

'Yes. His name is Liam.'

'He's a bonny lad.'

Laura smiled. 'I'm not going to disagree with that,' she told him.

The door opened again and Jon came in from the street. 'So you are doing as I suggested,' he said approvingly. 'Getting to know us before you start. Who have you met so far, Laura?'

'Just Denise and Tim,' she told him with a faster-beating heart.

'I would have introduced you to everyone myself. But as both Tim and I have been called out on emergency visits and there are patients waiting to be seen, I'll get Kathy, one of the practice nurses, to take over.

She's free at the moment, and Denise can keep an eye on Liam for you. When you've done the rounds I'll show you the apartment. OK?'

They seemed a friendly enough lot, Laura thought when she'd been introduced to everyone. Except for when she'd shaken hands with Alison Arkwright, the practice manager, and she'd said, 'Aren't you Harry Hewitt's daughter? I've seen you going to and from his house, yet I've never seen you around before. It was sad what happened to him.'

There was a hint of reproof in the comment and Laura thought that someone had her down for a negligent daughter. Unloved would be a better description, but her affairs were hers alone. If she'd already been coupled with her father, at least no one at the practice seemed to be aware of her past connections with Jon.

When she went back to Reception the waiting room was empty and when she knocked on Jon's door he called out, 'Come in, Laura, and take a seat.'

He smiled as she lowered herself into the chair at the other side of his desk, and said, 'We need to discuss your hours.'

She nodded.

'The surgery opens at eight-thirty each morning. The staff usually arrive any time between eight and half past. I realise that could be awkward for you, so suggest that your hours should be from nine o'clock in the morning to half past three in the afternoon when the primary school children come out. What do you think?'

'That would be fine. It's good of you to fit in with my responsibilities to Liam.'

He shrugged. 'Surely it doesn't surprise you. I have a child of my own, don't forget.'

'No. It doesn't surprise me at all,' she said quietly. 'Thank you, Jon.'

'Don't mention it,' he said, and got to his feet. 'So we will see you at nine o'clock on Monday morning, yes?'

He was obviously not intending to waste too much time on her, she thought, and rose to face him.

'Yes, you will. Shall we go and see the flat now?' she asked, and went to persuade a reluctant Liam to get off the rocking horse.

The flat above the surgery was spacious and nicely furnished with two bedrooms, sitting room, bathroom and a small kitchen.

Jon had been watching her expression as she'd looked around and now he asked, 'So, what do you think?'

'It's fine,' she said blithely. 'After my dad's place it's a palace.'

'So that's sorted, then. It will be just a matter of transferring your personal things. But what about your furniture in the house in Cornwall?'

'James Penrose is buying my house furnished, so there's no problem there.'

When she'd gone Jon sat gazing thoughtfully into space. Laura had questioned whether he was going to regret having her around him in such close proximity and he wondered what had brought that on.

It was good to have her back in the village again. Yet too much water had flowed under the bridge for things to ever be as they once had been. When he'd seen her standing on the back step of that ghastly house of her father's and discovered that she was a single parent like himself, he'd wanted to weep for all the lost years of their friendship.

Why hadn't she come back when she'd lost Freddie? he wondered, and knew the answer even as he asked himself the question. What had there been for her to come back to? As far as he was concerned he'd blown it after the way he'd forgotten her at university, and her father wouldn't have been pleased to have her back with the added encumbrance of a baby. It was no wonder she'd stayed put.

He'd made his impulsive job offer for two reasons— firstly because it had seemed like common sense when they needed some extra help at the surgery and Laura would have to earn a living in some way that would fit in with caring for Liam, and secondly because it would be good having her back in Heathermere once more.

If Laura had wanted to arrive at the practice on the Monday morning looking calm and elegant, it was not to be. Since she'd returned to the village Jon had only seen her in old cotton tops and jeans or shorts. So today she wanted to make a statement, wanted to let him see that she could look good when she made the effort.

In a smart navy suit with a white shirt, sheer stockings and moderately high-heeled shoes, she was calm and composed until Liam burst into tears at the door of the classroom and refused to go inside.

She was dismayed at his distress and as she tried to reassure him that there was nothing to be afraid of,

Laura thought he'd been so good since she'd brought him to Heathermere, maybe Liam was entitled to a moment of protest.

His teacher was sympathetic. 'Don't cry, Liam,' she coaxed, and added in an aside to Laura, 'Those who are apprehensive usually settle down once their mums have gone. If your little one doesn't, I'll give you a ring, but I'm sure he will be all right.'

'We've been living in Cornwall,' Laura told her, 'and have come back to where I was brought up. So Liam is having an unsettling time. He isn't usually like this.'

'That makes it perfectly understandable,' the teacher said, and taking him by the hand she led him gently inside, motioning for Laura to go as she did so.

Once out of sight it was her turn to weep and when she arrived at the practice for a briefing from Jon before she started work, her eyes were red-rimmed and there was a wet patch on the front of her shirt from Liam's tears.

'What's wrong, Laura?' Jon asked immediately.

She gave a rueful smile. 'Liam began to cry when we arrived at the school and I wasn't expecting it. He's not usually weepy, but of course it is a big thing for any child, their first day at school, and I *have* uprooted him from the only place he's ever known. He went in all right eventually with a very nice teacher and then it was my turn to get upset.' She looked down at the sodden handkerchief that she was holding in her hand. 'I'm sorry to turn up in such a state on my first morning here.'

'Don't apologise for caring,' he said, resisting the urge to reach out for her and offer the comfort of his arms. 'Go and have a cup of tea before you get bogged down with patients, and I'll see you when you've calmed down.'

She shook her head. 'I'm all right, Jon, thanks. I'm better being occupied, and I *am* here to work.'

Monday morning at any practice was one of the busiest times of the week, with the regulars and those who'd succumbed to some kind of health problem over the weekend adding to their numbers.

'All right. Whatever you say,' he agreed. 'It should have occurred to me to ask Abby to look out for Liam in the playground. Is he having school dinners?'

'Yes, and, please, don't cause Abby any embarrassment in front of her friends. I feel that we are causing enough disruption in your lives already. What does your mother think about me joining the practice?'

'She thinks it's a good idea.' He opened the door next to his. 'This will be your room, Laura. We've arranged a few consultations for you and once the waiting room is clear, I'll take you with me on my house calls.'

Laura followed him in and looked appreciatively around her new practice room. It was light and airy, with some well-tended plants on the windowsill.

'I'll show you the basics so you'll have got the hang of it before you start,' Jon said. 'By the time we get back from the house calls, it'll almost be time for you to pick Liam up.' He smiled at the anxiety that flitted across her face. 'I'm sure he'll have forgotten his upset of earlier, with all the new and exciting things that primary school children are involved in.'

'I hope so,' she said wryly, and went to settle herself behind the desk.

Her first patient of the day turned out to be the most interesting. Jessica Dinsdale was a smart seventy-five-year-old who looked much younger than her age.

Laura had brought herself up to date with the woman's bulky records over many years before she'd called her in and had been astounded at the number of unpleasant ailments she'd triumphed over—two major heart operations, gall-bladder removal, a hysterectomy and various other problems.

Today she had come with another serious health problem and was hardly coherent as she tried to explain what it was, because she couldn't stop yawning.

'I've had a stroke of some kind,' Jessica Dinsdale said between yawns. 'I was making a cup of tea late last night when the use went out of my left arm and leg. It only lasted a few moments but I was alarmed, and this morning I asked to see a doctor. Jon Emmerson was fully booked so they put me on your list.'

Laura nodded. 'I can understand you being alarmed, Mrs Dinsdale. Your records tell me that you've had a metal heart valve for almost thirty years and have been on warfarin all that time.'

At the end of another massive yawn her patient said, 'Call me Jessica, dear. Yes, that is so, and during all that time I've had to have my blood monitored to make sure that the warfarin isn't making it too thin. The possibility of a stroke has always been on my mind and last evening it was even more so.'

'How long have you been yawning in this manner?'

'Ever since it happened.'

When Laura sounded her heart, its beat was fast and irregular and Jessica asked, 'Will it be the warfarin that has caused this?'

Laura shook her head. 'No. Not at all. Warfarin is a wonderful drug. Thirty years is a long time to have lived with a metal replacement valve, and I see that many years before you were given the valve you were operated on for mitral stenosis, a blockage of the mitral valve that was eventually replaced. What did they use in those days to clear that sort of blockage?'

Jessica smiled. 'The surgeon used his finger to widen it fifty years ago.'

'Incredible! You're an amazing woman to have survived all the major surgery you've had. I'm going to ring for an ambulance to come here and take you to hospital. After yesterday's occurrence you need to be seen by someone in Neurology, who will probably send you for a CT scan.'

'What about the yawning?' Jessica asked. 'I just can't stop. It's so embarrassing.'

"I've done some specialising in neurology myself,' Laura told her, 'and there is an area at the bottom of the brain that controls yawning. It could be that you've had a small bleed there and that's what is causing it. Do you drive?'

'Yes. But I haven't driven here. I walked.'

'You should have asked for a visit,' she chided gently,

'and driving is out of the question for the time being, until they've sorted out what is going on inside your head. Do you live alone?'

'Yes.'

'Right. If you will take a seat in the waiting room the ambulance will be here shortly, and if you want to phone a relative the receptionist will sort that out for you.'

As Jessica raised herself slowly off the chair Laura said, 'One last question, and I hope you don't mind my asking it. Are you Jessica Dinsdale, the crime writer?'

The woman opposite smiled and nodded. 'Yes, I am.'

'I'm reading one of your books at the moment and enjoying it immensely.'

'Thank you. I need something to cheer me up,' Jessica said. 'My latest book is out soon. I'll let you have a signed copy if you like.'

'That would be lovely,' Laura told her. 'I don't get out much in the evenings as I have a young son, so I do quite a bit of reading.'

During the morning she kept wondering how Liam was faring and when it was time for her to go with Jon on house calls he said, as if reading her mind, 'We can drive past the school if you like. The children will have had their lunch by now and should be in the playground, so you might get a glimpse of Liam.'

'But supposing he's still upset,' she said doubt-fully. 'It will be worse if he sees me, and I'll be even more on edge.'

'I'm sure that he'll have settled in fine,' he said, 'and if that is the case, you'll be able to relax until it's time to pick him up. So shall we drive past slowly?'

Laura nodded. She couldn't say no to that, whatever might be the result.

Tears were threatening again and she fought them back. Someone was looking after her, considering her feelings, understanding what it was like to be a single parent, and incredibly it was Jon, who she'd worshipped from a distance all that time ago.

'There he is!' he said as they drove past the school gates, and when she looked Laura could see Liam's small fair head bobbing up and down as he chased around with the other children. And he wasn't crying.

'Do you feel better now?' Jon asked as they drove on.

'I most certainly do,' she said, smiling across at him from the passenger seat, and he thought that she looked more like the old Laura in that moment, happy and relaxed, instead of sombre and withdrawn.

'So now that your mind is at rest, shall we go and see what ails those who couldn't make it to the surgery?' he said easily.

'Yes, of course,' she replied, serious once more. 'I don't want to be a liability, Jon. I will pull my weight in the practice and am sorry that I've been such a wet lettuce on my first day.'

'Don't worry about it. You're with someone who's been there already. On Abby's first day at school there weren't any tears, but when it was over she announced that she didn't like it and wouldn't be going again. It was quite some time before she got used to the idea that she didn't have a choice.'

He was pulling up outside the village's fish and chip shop and she said, 'It's rather early for lunch, isn't it?'

'We're here to see the owner's mother who lives with him above the shop,' he explained, 'so don't get carried away by the appetising smells. Do you remember Kelvin Cartwright, who was always pulling your plaits at school until I dotted him one?'

She laughed. 'Yes. How could I forget him?'

He raised his eyebrows comically. 'Well, he owns this "plaice".'

Her laughter increased and he thought how great it was to see her unwinding as she said, 'It sounds a bit fishy to me.'

'His mother has heart problems and he's brought her to live with him so that he can keep an eye on her. Mrs Cartwright is waiting for a pacemaker to be fitted. She sometimes has periods of complete memory loss and the cardiology department thinks it is when the blood isn't getting to her brain because of an irregular heartbeat.

'If you remember, she was on school dinners when we were young, but now she's very frail. I doubt you will recognise her. Kelvin and his wife are doing the best they can for her, which isn't easy with a business to run.'

The tormentor of her youth was busy behind the counter, getting ready for opening, but when he saw them he wiped his hands and came round.

'Hello, Laura,' he said with a sheepish grin. 'I'd heard you were back. It must seem like old times, the two of you together. The grapevine also said that you're working at the surgery.'

'Yes, this is my first day,' she told him. 'Good to see you again, Kelvin. I understand that your mother isn't well.'

He sighed. 'Yes. Don't expect her to know you. We take it in turns to be with her. My wife is up there now. Otherwise she gets frightened when her memory blanks out. It comes and goes. We're hoping that she'll improve when the pacemaker has been fitted.'

Jon hadn't spoken while they'd been chatting, but now he said, 'We'll go up then, Kelvin. By the way, I've been on to the hospital again to see if I can get your mother's operation brought forward. They might be in touch with you in the very near future so be prepared.'

CHAPTER THREE

BOTH Jon and the shop owner were wrong in assuming that Kelvin's mother wouldn't know who Laura was. She was gazing through the window of what appeared to be a bedsitting room, looking down at the main street of the village where people were going about their business, and she turned slowly when Jon said, 'Hello, Mrs Cartwright. How are you?'

He saw immediately that they'd caught her on one of her better days as, without replying, she said, 'Laura? Laura Hewitt!'

Laura stepped forward and took her frail hand in hers. Alice Cartwright had been a buxom woman when she'd last seen her, but illness and old age had brought about a great change in her.

'Hello, Mrs Cartwright. I'm Laura Cavendish now,' she told her gently, 'and I've come back to live in the village with my little boy.'

Kelvin's mother nodded. 'That is good. Will you bring him to see me?'

Laura smiled. 'Yes, of course.'

Jon had moved across to speak to Alice's daughter-in-law, who was hovering anxiously in the background.

'She seems better today, Sandra,' he said, wondering why she had asked him to visit.

'Yes, I know,' Sandra told him. 'But earlier this morning Mum was having difficulty breathing.'

'Any chest pains?'

'No. Just trouble breathing, like an asthma attack. She's got enough to cope with already without that.'

'Indeed she has,' he agreed. 'Though she seems all right now. I'll check her over. We can't be too careful.'

After he'd had Alice breathing in and out several times Jon put away his stethoscope and said to Sandra, 'Her breathing *is* shallow. If you could bring Alice to the surgery I'll get one of the practice nurses to do a spirometry test.'

'What's that?' she wanted to know.

'Alice will be asked to breathe out into the mouthpiece of a spirometer and it will produce a graph that helps to show if any kind of lung disease such as asthma is present. It's a simple enough procedure, nothing that will alarm her, and if the signs are there I will probably prescribe an inhaler.'

He glanced across to where Alice was still chatting to Laura. 'The fact that Alice does have days like this is encouraging. If we can sort out the irregular heartbeat that momentarily stops blood getting to the brain, the memory loss might lessen, but don't get your hopes up too much, Sandra.'

"I won't,' she promised, 'and thank you for coming, Dr Emmerson.'

Driving towards their next call, Jon sighed. 'You've just seen Alice on a good day,' he told Laura. 'Sometimes she doesn't know me, but today she certainly knew who you were.'

She smiled. 'Yes, she did. It's good to be meeting people who once were so familiar to me. They've changed, of course, but so have I…and so have you, Jon.'

'Responsibilities do that,' he said wryly. 'I hadn't a care in the world until I knew I was going to be a father. I was so intent on enjoying myself that I shut you out, didn't I?'

'You didn't owe me anything.'

'Yes. I did, Laura. We'd been friends for years and I behaved as if we were strangers.'

'Like we are now?'

'Is that how it feels?'

'Yes, but it's not surprising, is it? We've been travelling different paths for a long time. I married Freddie, and your future had already been mapped out with your resolve to bring up Abby yourself. Though I would have expected you to have found someone else by now. Surely there are lots of women who'd love to marry a man with a ready-made family.'

'And what about lots of men wanting to marry a woman in that situation,' he asked whimsically. 'Does that apply?'

She smiled and again he was reminded of how she'd once been. The glance from eyes as blue as the Cornish sea that had taken her husband wasn't as strained and wary as it had been.

"I've never had the time or inclination to find out,' she said, and wondered what he would say if she told him that she'd never forgotten *him*. That though they'd been out of touch for a long time he had a special place in her heart and always would have. Nothing was going to change that, and nothing was going to change the feeling that he would run a mile if he knew.

'Same here,' he said. 'I've never had the inclination either.'

Maybe, she thought, but not for the same reason. He hadn't known the pangs of a teenage crush that had never come to anything.

Jon's life was safe and secure. He had it all mapped out. Yet he'd found her employment and somewhere to live, and she was grateful. Even though she knew it had only been for old time's sake. Or maybe because he'd remembered how he'd dropped her the moment they'd gone to medical school and had felt guilty.

'We've been asked to call at one of the sheep farms,' he said, turning onto a steep road that led to the moors and the magnificent peaks beyond. 'Martin Pritchard, who owns the place, has an ongoing relationship with my mother.'

'Really?'

He was smiling. 'Purely platonic. Martin is a grumpy old thing, but has a soft heart underneath. When a ewe has a sickly lamb in the spring he sends it down to her to be nursed. She has a small grazing area at the bottom of the garden and at the moment there are three sheep on it that she has reared.

'They are the first thing Abby goes to look at when she comes home from school. She's seen them grow from lambs and has named them Baa, Lambkin and Curly.'

'That's lovely,' she said. 'Can I bring Liam to see them some time?'

'Yes, of course,' he replied easily. 'Whenever you want. It will seem strange but nice, watching our children grow up together like we did, won't it?'

Laura nodded but made no comment, and Jon thought that she was probably remembering how she'd become surplus to requirements once they'd gone to university.

It was going through her mind that maybe they were moving too fast. She could be asking for more heartache and end up fretting on the sidelines of Jon's life once more. But it would be delightful for their children to get to know each other. It was going to seem very strange to Liam on his first day at school if he'd never met any of the other children.

Was she being fair to him? she wondered. If she'd gone back to Cornwall, as had been her intention before she'd met Jon again, everything would have been much simpler. But just the sight of him had made her come to life again and she hadn't felt like that in a long time.

'And so what is wrong with Martin Pritchard?' she asked, bringing her mind back to the reason they were driving towards the moors.

'When Martin phoned the surgery this morning he said that he'd been having minor pain around the navel and that now it had moved to the lower right-hand side of his stomach and it was intense.'

'Sounds as if it could be appendicitis.'

'Mmm. It does,' he agreed. 'And it's sometimes a tricky condition to diagnose. I once nearly lost a patient because he didn't know that in such a situation an inflamed appendix is at its most dangerous when the pain goes away. He thought it had just been a gastric upset.' He pulled up outside a rambling farmhouse. 'Martin is a tough old guy. He runs the farm with the help of a couple of local people, and I don't remember him ever having anything wrong with him before, but there's always a first time.'

Ann Stephens, a bustling fifty-year-old from the village who drove up each day to keep the place tidy, opened the door to them and said, 'I've just arrived and found Martin really poorly, Dr Emmerson. He's in a lot of pain.'

Jon nodded. 'Lead us to him then, Ann,' he told her.

As the two doctors followed her into a cluttered sitting room she said, 'It's nice to have you among us again, Laura.'

'Thanks,' she replied. 'It's good to be back.'

If Jon had heard her, he gave no indication. He was striding across to where the farmer was slumped in an easy chair, ashen-faced and groaning.

As Ann made a discreet exit Jon said, 'I need to feel your stomach, Martin. Can you loosen your trousers?'

The farmer did so with difficulty and cried out when Jon felt the area where the pain was located.

'I'm going to ask our new doctor to examine you now,' he said. 'Two heads are better than one, though I've a good idea what's wrong. You remember Laura, don't you?'

'Aye,' Martin grunted. 'Harry Hewitt's daughter, aren't you?'

'Yes,' she told him, 'and I'll be as gentle as I can.'

When she'd finished feeling the lower abdomen of the sick man she nodded without speaking and Jon said, 'I'm going to do a further examination, Martin. We think the pain is coming from your appendix.'

When he'd finished his expression was grave. 'Can you phone for an ambulance, Laura?' he asked. 'Impress upon them that it's urgent.'

'I can't leave the farm,' Martin protested weakly. 'There's the chickens to feed and a couple of horses to exercise. The sheep are out on the moorland so they're no trouble at this time of the year, but—'

'Your farmhand can see to those sorts of things,' Jon told him firmly.

'The most important thing is to get you to hospital before your appendix bursts.'

Laura had made the call he'd asked for and said, 'The emergency services are on their way, Mr Pritchard. I'll go and ask Ann if she'll pack you a bag with a few essentials so that there will be no delay when they get here.'

When the ambulance had taken the suffering farmer to A and E, the two doctors left Ann to keep an eye on things and proceeded to their next call, which was to the home of a small boy with an inflamed throat that had all the signs of tonsilitis.

He was enjoying having Laura with him, Jon was thinking. She was quietly efficient, ready to keep in the background but there when called upon. He wondered how she was seeing her first foray into village health care.

When they got back to the practice Tim had just returned from his home visits and while the three doctors stopped for a break and a quick bite Laura went to have a peep at the schoolyard again during the afternoon break.

A reassuring glimpse of Liam, with Abby hovering protectively beside him, sent her back to the surgery with a lighter heart, and as she ate a sandwich and drank a quick coffee her spirits lifted.

Life was going to be good, she thought. Better than she'd ever thought it could be. Both Liam and herself had had hurdles to face that morning—Liam his first day at school, and for herself joining the practice. There had been a feeling of unreality about it all, but it had gone well and she was happy.

'I don't need to ask where you've been.' Jon said when she'd got back from her surveillance of the schoolyard. 'Was Liam all right?'

She smiled. 'Yes, he was fine. It seemed as if Abby had taken him under her wing, which was sweet of her. I suppose you think I'm fussing a lot.'

'Nothing of the kind. I was just as bad on Abby's first day. I should have guessed she might seek him out. When she knew he had no father she amazed me by saying, "And I have no mummy. So we're not like other children, are we?"'

'What did you say to that?' she asked, as a small lump formed in her throat.

He smiled. 'I told her that because of it they were loved twice as much, and it's true, isn't it?'

'Yes, it's true,' she agreed, and for a fleeting moment thought it was a pity they couldn't do something about the gaps in their children's lives, but the sea would freeze over before Jon ever thought along those lines. She wasn't gorgeous Kezia with the come-to-bed eyes, but neither was she a woman who could desert her child.

She adored Liam, and if she never did anything else that was praiseworthy, she was making sure that he had a happy and secure childhood. That he knew he was cherished above all else. Like herself, he had lost a parent, but unlike what had happened to her, he was loved all the more because of it.

Laura was waiting at the school gates, along with the other mothers. School was over and the children were about to come streaming out when Marjorie appeared beside her.

'So how has the day gone, Laura?' she asked with a smile. 'It's been a new beginning for both Liam and yourself, hasn't it.'

Laura smiled back at the woman who'd been the nearest thing to a mother she'd known during her childhood days and said, 'I've enjoyed every moment at the surgery with Jon and Tim, but Liam wasn't happy when I left him this morning and he's been on my mind all day. Abby was with him in the afternoon break when I went to have a quick peek at him, and I did feel better after that.'

'She's a loving child,' Marjorie said. 'She wasn't sure about him being around at first, but when she knew that they both only had one parent, our little girl felt protective of him. Jon adores her and so do I. Sometimes I wish she had a loving stepmother, but Jon doesn't seem prepared to take any risks on that score.

'He says she is too precious to be in the care of any other woman than myself, and that she's happy enough as she is, but I worry for *him*. It's a lonely life for any man, bringing up a child without a mother, and I'm sure that it is no joke either when the boot is on the other foot and there's no father.'

'It isn't always a bundle of laughs, for sure,' Laura said, 'but Jon and I are blessed with our children, aren't we? Does he ever hear from Kezia?' she asked, not sure what she wanted to hear.

Marjorie shook her head. 'Never a word. What's more, he doesn't want to. It is as if she's disappeared off the face of the earth. She was young and couldn't face up to the responsibility of parenthood. Yet so was he, and having to take full responsibility for a baby hadn't been how he'd had his life planned. It soon brought him down to earth, but he's done it.'

At that moment the school doors were flung open, the children came pouring out and Liam was coming towards her, eyes blue as her own big in his face as he gazed up at Abby walking beside him.

When he saw her waiting at the gate he ran forward and threw himself into her arms, and as Laura looked at Marjorie and her granddaughter, smiling across at them above his fair head, she felt for the first time as if she had really come home.

Jon had found her a job and a place to live, but she knew he was just going through the motions, helping her sort her life out, and the last thing she wanted was pity. She'd been a single parent for five long years and knew how to cope. It was just unfortunate that they'd met again under such circumstances. That it had taken her father's funeral to bring her back to the village and the man who'd once held her heart in his hands without even knowing it.

He rang that evening and there was a lift to his voice as he said, 'So we have a good report of Liam's first day I believe. I've heard all about it from Abby. They seem to be getting on very well.'

'Yes, they do,' she told him, her pleasure at the thought equalling his.

'But I still can't help feeling that Liam and I are butting into your lives.'

There was silence at the other end of the line for a moment and then he said coolly, 'Do you have to be so independent, Laura? Can't you see that I realise what a pain I was all that time ago, and because I got my priorities wrong by being selfish and uncaring, I want to make up for it.'

'Yet you never made any effort to get in touch over the years.'

'The same applies to you, and do you think I would have gone barging back into your life because I needed a shoulder to cry on when you were married to Freddie? I thought we'd picked up some of the threads again today at the surgery. But if you think that you're being patronised, maybe I was wrong, and at the risk of adding to that feeling I'm ringing to tell you that I've got a decorator coming to brighten up the apartment for you tomorrow. He's bringing some colour charts with him so that you can choose whatever appeals to you. How long before you have to be out of your father's house?'

'I've got until the end of next week.'

'Fine. He should be finished by then. You saw that

the place is newly furnished, so what do you intend to do with your father's furniture? Put it in storage?'

'No. I'll send everything to be auctioned, apart from a few pieces of my mother's jewellery that he'd always kept.'

'Right,' he said briskly. 'So unless you decide to flee back to Cornwall during the night because I'm too interfering, I'll see you in the morning, Laura.'

'I don't think that at all,' she protested, but the line was dead. Jon had gone back to whatever he did on summer evenings after Abby was asleep, and she was left feeling ashamed at having made him think she didn't appreciate all that he was doing for her.

They'd always been straight with each other. Until they'd gone to medical school, that was, and now, as far as Jon was concerned, they were back on the old footing. But he wasn't having to keep a tight hold on his feelings whenever they were together, like she was.

In his apartment above the surgery, quiet now that Abby was asleep, Jon was gazing out of the window. Since his daughter had been born no woman had caught his imagination. The practice and his role of single father had kept him fully occupied. But now, amazingly, Laura was back in his life, and all the time he was remembering what they'd said and done together. How they'd laughed at the same things, liked the same things, looked forward to roaming the fields together, playing down by the river, and then moving into adolescence together. It had all been so uncomplicated until they'd gone to university.

Time had changed them both. His responsibilities controlled his life, and losing Freddie had taken the zest out of Laura. For a crazy moment he wished he could turn back the clock. When he'd discovered that Freddie had died just after Liam's birth and she'd been alone ever since, he'd been aghast and desperate to make up for his past neglect.

The yearning to see the old Laura back again was consuming him. The Laura with hair as gold as the corn at harvest time. Who'd saved all her smiles for *him*, and could climb any tree that he could.

But after the conversation they'd just had it seemed as if he might be going the wrong way about it. Chipping away at her independence in his eagerness to help.

The next morning after Liam had gone into school without any sign of reluctance Laura presented herself at the surgery once more.

Jon and Tim were already seeing their patients as the practice opened at half past eight, so any chance of making peace with Jon from the night before would have to wait until they went on house calls. But they did speak briefly when Jon came to the door of his room to call in the next patient and saw her arriving.

'The decorator has already been and left the brochures if you want to pop up to the apartment in the lunch-hour,' he told her.

'Yes, I'll do that.' she agreed with a smile that she hoped would take away the chill of their last conversation, but it was wasted. Jon had turned his attention to the teenage boy hobbling painfully out of the waiting room towards him.

Later in the morning as they drove off the forecourt of the old stone building on the main street of the village he said, 'Ann Stephens rang earlier to say that Martin has had an appendicectomy, so we weren't wrong about that, were we?'

'No, it would seem not,' she replied. 'I felt sorry for him when he was so anxious about leaving the farm. It's one of the things that I've always dreaded. Something happening to me and Liam being left in the care of someone else, maybe strangers.'

'I can understand that,' he said soberly. 'I'm fortunate to have my mother close by for that sort of eventuality. But, Laura, I hope you know that now you're back where you belong, you have only to call and I'll be there, and so will anyone else who knows you.'

'Yes, I do know that,' she said, 'and I'm grateful.'

He took his gaze off the road for a second to observe her expression and said with a tightness in his tone, 'You don't have to be grateful. Happy and secure is how I want you to feel.'

She didn't reply to that. Instead, she said, 'About last night when you phoned. I felt I'd annoyed you in some way. If I did, I'm sorry. You've been so good to me and…'

He was exasperated now. It was there in his voice as he said, 'We have a lot to catch up on, for goodness' sake! I want us to be as we were before… good friends. I know whose fault it is that the friendship lapsed, but we've been given a second chance and I won't be making the same mistake twice.'

She wondered what he would say if she told him that she didn't want to be just 'good friends'. That the more she saw of him, the more she wanted from him, and he wouldn't want to give it because she was just Laura.

But she couldn't hurt him by rejecting his wishes for a fresh start. It was turning out to be a time of new beginnings all round, with Liam at school, her medical career moving in a different direction and, most surprising of all, Jon back in her life. If good friends was all that he had in mind, she would be crazy not to take what was on offer.

'Of course I want us to be friends again,' she said softly. 'What happened in the past doesn't matter any more. It's the present that counts.'

He was smiling now, regretting his impatience. Being with Laura again gave him a good feeling. He was the one who should be grateful. He'd been living too long without female company of his own age.

Laura went up to the apartment on her own in the lunchhour as Jon had been waylaid by a salesman from one of the big pharmaceutical firms and she was anxious to view the place again and pick up the colour charts.

When the door swung open the place was in darkness as the curtains were still drawn, and her hand went out to grope for a light switch. There was nothing immediately obvious so she stepped into the darkness of the hallway and went flying over a large can of paint that the decorator must have left.

Jon had finished talking to the salesman and was halfway up the stairs when he heard her fall. He took the last few steps two at a time, flicked on the light switch, which had been just a couple of inches beyond her reach, and found Laura struggling to her feet, with blood oozing down the side of her face.

'I hit my head on something,' she said shakily as his arms went round her, and then fainted.

'Oh, Laura, sweetheart,' he murmured gently, aware of the limpness of her soft curves as he pushed open the door of the main bedroom with his foot and laid her gently on the bed. He'd had no idea that the decorator had left a big tin of undercoat in the hallway, he thought raggedly.

It had only been a couple of hours ago that she'd voiced her fears of anything happening that would stop her from looking after Liam and here she was, bleeding and fainting all in the space of minutes.

Jon took her hand in his and felt her pulse. It seemed regular enough and at that moment she moaned and opened her eyes. 'What happened?' she asked groggily. 'Did I faint?'

'Yes,' he told her. 'Stay where you are for a moment. Don't try to move. I'm going to go downstairs to get something to stop the bleeding. You hurt your face when you fell, most likely banged it against the hall table, and the shock of the fall made you faint.'

When he'd bathed her face and put an antiseptic dressing on the cut, he ran his fingers gently across her cheek and asked, 'No broken bones or other injuries that you haven't mentioned?'

She was wearing a short-sleeved cotton shirt and a big bruise was appearing on her arm just above the elbow, but she shook her head at the question and said, 'No. I seem to be able to move everything, though, no doubt, I'll have more bruises tomorrow.'

'I'll take you home,' he offered. 'You need to rest.'

She shook her head and raised herself upright on the bedcover. 'No, Jon, I'm all right. Just a bit shaken up, that's all. I must be there to pick Liam up after school, whatever happens, as it's only his second day. As for the colour charts, I might as well take them with me, having almost knocked myself out in the process of getting them.'

'I didn't know the decorator had left the tin of paint there,' he told her regretfully, 'and the light switch in the hall is quite a way in from the front door. I'll have to take better care of you in future.'

He wasn't going to mention that he would rather the first time he'd held her in his arms had been on a less fraught occasion. In that moment he'd been amazed at the anxious tenderness that had overwhelmed him on seeing her in such a state.

When they went downstairs Laura insisted that she was all right to assist with the antenatal clinic that Jon and one of the practice nurses took on a Tuesday afternoon, but he wouldn't have any of it.

"You can sit and watch, and that is it,' he told her. 'And I'm going to ask one of the receptionists to make you a cup of hot, sweet tea.'

It was happening again Laura thought wryly. She was at a disadvantage and Jon was taking charge. And how odd that on the only occasion she'd ever been in his arms, she'd known very little about it.

As she waited for Liam once more outside the school gates it suddenly hit her how near she'd been to the thing she dreaded. If she'd been seriously hurt in the fall she wouldn't have been there to meet him, and what would she have done then?

But even as the dismaying thought came to mind there was comfort to be had in knowing that she wasn't alone any more. Jon was close by, and if he never ever touched her again, she would get by somehow.

CHAPTER FOUR

JON came to check on Laura later that evening and when she opened the door to him in the summer dusk he answered the question in her eyes by saying, 'Abby is staying at my mother's for the night. She does that sometimes.

'I've come to see how you're feeling and if you'd like me to stay the night in case you have any after-effects. That was some fall and I feel I should keep my eye on you, as I am your GP.'

'I would love to tell you that's an offer I can't refuse,' she told him. 'But I'd be trading on your good nature. I admit that I'm stiff and sore and have a headache, but that's all, and I'm sure that you can find better things to do with a free evening.'

'Such as?'

'I don't know, do I? What do you usually do?'

'It happens so rarely I can't remember,' he told her with a smile. 'So if you don't require my services, how about inviting me in for a coffee?'

'Yes, of course,' she said, throwing the door open wide and thinking at the same time that she must be crazy to pass up the chance of being under the same roof as Jon for the night. Even though she would be asleep upstairs and he would be bedded down on the sofa.

She thought she knew why he'd made the offer. It was because he felt responsible for her having an accident on the surgery premises, even though he hadn't been the one who'd left the paint can there.

Jon went into the sitting room, glancing at her as she went into the kitchen. The last thing likely to occur to her was that his concern was tinged with a sudden awareness of her that he'd never experienced before, and that, having felt it, he'd been eager to see her again to discover if it was still there...and it was.

Before she'd just been Laura. Part of his growing-up and teenage years. If anyone had asked him to describe her, he wouldn't have known where to begin, so used had he been to her presence.

But it was different now. She was her own person. Liam's mother, and a doctor like himself, with a delicate attractiveness that he was becoming more aware of all the time.

What she thought of *him* after all this time he didn't know. Laura had only sought him out once of her own free will since she'd come back to Heathermere. It had been the night when she'd found him at his mother's house, and told him she had a buyer for the cottage in Cornwall, and would like to accept his offer of employment at the practice.

In the kitchen, making coffee, Laura had no idea of the direction of his thoughts. She was still trying to come to terms with Jon wanting to stay the night because he was worried about her. It was pleasant to be the subject of his concern, but she wasn't going to read anything into the gesture that wasn't there.

When she went into the sitting room with the coffee-cups he said, 'Do you remember how we used to go to the midsummer fair that came to Heathermere every year when we were young?'

'Yes, of course I do.'

'Well, it still comes. The sequence has never been broken. It will be here for two days on Friday and Saturday. How about we take the children?'

'That's a nice idea,' she said slowly, a little taken aback by the suggestion. 'Liam would love that. Especially if Abby is going to be there. He talks about her all the time.'

'She's the same about him,' he told her, and there was regret in his voice.

'Abby pretends he's her little brother, which just goes to show how she wishes she wasn't an only child. But I'm afraid there is nothing I can do about that.'

'That's not quite true, is it?' she pointed out.

'What do you mean?'

'Your mother would like you to find yourself a wife.'

'Yes. I know. Yet I can't fall in love to order, and after my experience with Kezia I wouldn't settle for anything less than the real thing. An all-consuming love that would embrace Abby, too. But I don't have much time for socialising. I've managed without a woman in my life so far, and my daughter seems happy enough, even though she hasn't got any brothers and sisters.'

Laura nodded, wishing she hadn't said anything.

'So, back to the fair,' he continued. 'How about we call for you both after lunch on Saturday? Then when our young ones have had their fill of it, take them to eat at one of the fast-food places that children seem to like so much.'

'Yes. Why not? It sounds like fun,' she told him, eyes sparkling at the thought of prime time with Jon and the children.

He didn't stay long. When he'd drunk his coffee he said, 'If you won't let me be the night nurse, I'll be off, Laura. At least I can let you have an early night. I don't know if you've looked in the mirror since you came home, but that is a beauty of a black eye you've got. Promise you'll ring me if you don't feel well. I can be over in minutes.'

'I'll be fine,' she assured him, still thinking she was insane not to take advantage of his concern. Yet she couldn't do that. Jon was going through the motions of the caring employer and she couldn't fault him on it. But she'd turned up for work at the practice in Cornwall and looked after Liam many a time when she'd felt a lot worse than she did now.

'You are a very independent woman, Laura Hewitt.' he said.

'Cavendish,' she reminded him, with the sparkle still there.

'All right then, Cavendish. But I suppose it isn't surprising. You've had to be, haven't you?'

'Mmm, I guess so,' she replied. 'But I was a much stronger person than the one you knew when I lost Freddie. I'd begun to make a life of my own before I married him and he loved the new me because I was no longer prepared to put up with the way my father treated me.

'If I'd been like my old self when he drowned, I don't know how I would have survived, but as well as being more positive I had the greatest reason of all to face up to what had happened. Liam was just six months old when Freddie was taken from us.'

He nodded and said with a sombre smile, 'So do I need to remember that I am dealing with the new you?'

'Yes, I suppose so. But there is a lot of the old me still there as well.'

In the way my heartbeat quickens every time you are near she wanted to tell him, *and how I seem to just exist from one moment to the next because I am realising that I still care for you. That my feelings for you that I thought had completely gone during my happy years with Freddie are now taking over my life again.*

When he'd gone she locked up and went slowly up the stairs, bemused by many thoughts, and uppermost among them was Jon's suggestion that they take the children to the fair. It was something to really look forward to. For one thing it would give her the opportunity to get to know Abby, who in her own sweet young way was helping Liam to settle into his new life more than anyone.

One thing she didn't want to dwell on was Jon's description of what he would want out of a marriage. She would want the same. But it hurt too much to think that if he ever did consider it, he wouldn't be looking in her direction. Even if she filled her wardrobe with fash-

ionable clothes, had her hair restyled and a beauty treat-
ment, she would still be Laura Hewitt to him.

Before Saturday there was the rest of the week to be got
through with the children at school and the doctors ful-
filling their function at the practice. In the midst of it
Laura had chosen colour schemes for the apartment and
every time she went up there she was conscious of the
two front doors facing each other on the landing.

She wanted to be near Jon and was getting her wish,
she thought, but would it prove to be too near? They were
together down at the surgery and would be only feet
away up above it. It could prove to be a painful pleasure.

As patients came and went she found herself facing
the local hairdresser across her desk one morning.
Sharon Smith had found a lump in her breast and was
white-faced with dread.

When Laura had finished examining her she said,
'Sharon, there is a small swelling there, but it could be
lots of things besides cancer. It could be a calcium
deposit or a benign cyst, so don't start thinking the worst
until you've had some tests. The hospital will do a biopsy
and X-rays. Try to keep calm until you have a result.'

'I've been working hard to build the salon up into a
profitable business,' Sharon wailed, 'and just as I'm beginning to see some progress, this happens.'

'Yes, I know,' Laura said sympathetically, 'but, as
I've just said, don't jump to conclusions until you know
you have something to worry about. You won't have to
wait long for an appointment and in the meantime carry
on with your life as usual. Are you married?'

'Not yet. I'm engaged and we've set the wedding date for later in the year.'

'You'll make a lovely bride. Don't let this scare take away the anticipation of your wedding day.'

When she'd gone Laura rang the hospital to make an appointment for her before calling in the next patient. Once that was sorted she decided that the next time she was passing the salon she would book an appointment to have her hair cut and restyled on Saturday morning. She wasn't expecting Jon to be bowled over when he saw her, but at least *she* would get a buzz from it.

She was wrong about his reaction. When she opened the door to him and Abby early on Saturday afternoon he said, 'Wow! Your golden mop has never looked so, er...'

'Tidy?' she questioned wryly. 'Is that the word you were searching for?'

'No. It wasn't. I was going to say fantastic.'

Sharon had certainly displayed her skills with the unruly golden 'mop', as Jon had just described it, and now it hung smooth and shining just below her ears.

Without giving her time to reply to the compliment, he said, 'So are we ready to go?' With a glance at Abby and Liam, waiting impatiently at the gate, he added, 'The children are.'

The fair was like it had always been, bright, noisy and a magnet to young and old alike. When they went on the dodgems Liam surprised them by saying 'I want to be in Dr Jon's car.'

Not to be outdone Abby said shyly, 'Can I come in yours, Dr Cavendish?'

'Of course you can,' Laura told her, 'and, Abby, my name is Laura. You don't have to call me Dr Cavendish.'

'And, young man, my name is Jon,' he told Liam. That having been sorted, they paid for a couple of cars and went whizzing round and round to delighted cries from the children.

Then it was the Caterpillar ride, and as Abby cuddled up to Laura in the semi-darkness it was like getting to know a daughter she'd never had. Seated beside Jon, she could see that Liam was taking it all in his stride, with the occasional glance at the man beside him.

Was this therapy or madness? Laura wondered. Showing the children glimpses of the mother and father figures they'd never known. Whatever it was, they were a happy quartet as they wandered among the sideshows and amusements. It was only when hunger surfaced that Abby and Liam were ready to leave the fair.

It was the same at the fast-food place, Liam sitting next to Jon and Abby beside Laura, and the children chattered happily as they tucked into their meals.

'We have so much in common, don't we?' Jon said after they had finished their meal and were leaving the restaurant. 'The children, the job, the village that we both love, and soon we're going to be living next door to each other. Do you think you are going to find me too suffocating?'

The answer to that was a simple *No! Never!* But she felt that he was just making conversation and would be dumbfounded if that was her reply, so it was a casual answer to a casual question that he got.

'I'll let you know if I do,' she told him airily, and he was left to think that the feeler he'd just put out to discover how she saw him now that he was back in her life hadn't worked.

It was the middle of the evening and time to go their separate ways. The children were past their bedtimes but showing no signs of tiredness and Jon said, 'Come back to my place, Laura. You've not seen where Abby and I live yet. The children can have their bedtime drink together and I'll make something for us.'

Reluctant for the day to end, she smiled. 'Yes. I'd like to see your home.'

His answering smile was wry. 'You will, no doubt, see the absence of a woman's touch, but not where Abby is concerned. She chose her own bedroom furnishings and pink is the word. Lots of it. We have a comfortable sitting room and for the rest of it, well, it's basic, but we like it.'

Jon's description of the home he'd made for Abby and himself didn't do it justice, Laura thought when she saw inside. It was comfortably furnished, admittedly without a lot of ornaments and pictures but, having lived in her father's gloomy rented house for the last few weeks, it was hard to fault it.

When Abby asked shyly if Laura would like to see her bedroom, she said immediately, 'Yes. I'd love to.' She was enjoying getting to know Jon's daughter and hoped that after today Abby would see her as someone she could talk to.

'Oh!' she exclaimed when Abby opened the door. "What a pretty room.' And it was. As Jon had said there was lots of pink, but pink was a young girl's colour, and there was pride in the eyes of the child standing beside her as she showed her round the room that held all her treasures.

When Laura had finished admiring everything, Abby surprised her by saying, 'My daddy says that you and he used to play together when you were young, like Liam and I do. But that you went away when I was born. Why was that?'

Laura said gently, 'Well, your daddy had met your mummy and then you were on the way, so we didn't see so much of each other while that was happening, and then I married Liam's daddy and we went to live in Cornwall. But now we are back, and we are going to be friends, you and I. Would you like that?'

'Yes,' Abby told her with her confidence restored. 'And can Liam come round to play sometimes?'

'Of course, but you will need to ask your daddy first.'

When they went downstairs Jon observed her questioningly and Laura said immediately, 'Abby's bedroom is lovely, and to think that she chose everything herself.'

'Yes, indeed,' he replied with the question still there in his glance, and when the children went across the landing into the rooms that she and Liam would soon be occupying he asked, 'What has she been saying to you?'

'She asked me why I went away when she was born.'

He groaned. 'Abby asked me who you were and I tried to answer as sensibly as possible by telling her we were brought up together and then you moved away around the time she was born. It never occurred to me that she might think it was something to do with her. Let's face it, only you know why you rushed off and married Freddie.'

She frowned. 'I didn't rush into anything. We were happy together. If you are hinting that I made an unsuitable marriage, I would have thought you'd be the last one to be going on about unsuitable relationships,' she reminded him coolly, and thought they were ruining the last moments of what had been an idyllic day.

'I don't want to quarrel with you, Laura,' he said. 'But you are not aware that when you appeared out of the blue Abby hoped that you were the mother that she's never seen come to look for her. I'm not sure where she got that idea from, but she knows that her mother hasn't been around since she was a baby and maybe she connected your going away with Kezia's absence and thought you were one and the same.

'Or it might be simply that she wishes you were her mother. She doesn't ask about her an awful lot, but whenever she does I try to answer her questions truthfully. It was a painful moment when I had to dash her hopes with regard to you.'

'How sad,' she breathed.

'Yes,' he agreed sombrely. 'So maybe I painted the wrong picture for her. If I did, I hope you'll forgive me.'

As her anger fled she told him softly, 'I can forgive you anything, Jon. I'm just so sorry that your beautiful child should have had to suffer such a disappointment. How Kezia could bear to leave her behind I will never know. If Abby were mine I would never want to leave her side.' She sighed. 'What would you do if Kezia ever reappeared?'

He sighed. 'I don't know. Kezia and myself are long over. But she is Abby's mother. A poor one, but nevertheless that is what she is and I could never turn Abby against her if she had the nerve to come claiming the rights that she gave up all that time ago. One day when Abby is older she will want to know what it's all about, and I will explain what happened in the kindest way I can.'

He managed a smile. 'And in the meantime she is opening up to you. Liam she already adores. It's a joy to see them together.'

At that moment the children came back and as Laura and Liam prepared to leave Jon said in a low voice, 'It's been a great day, hasn't it, even though it did end on a more serious note?'

'Yes, it has,' she told him with her sparkle back. 'I haven't been so happy in ages.'

'That is all I want to hear,' he said, and gave her a swift hug.

On seeing it Abby did the same to a red-faced Liam and the two doctors exchanged smiles above their heads.

Laura spent the rest of the weekend preparing for the move. It was mostly packing clothes and toys and objects they'd accumulated since their return. The decorator would be finished by Tuesday. Her father's belongings were going to auction the following day, and that evening she and Liam would take up residence above the surgery.

Uneasiness kept coming over her every time she thought of what she was about to undertake. Would she be able to cope with the closeness of the arrangement without giving herself away?

Saturday had been wonderful. Even the misunderstanding at the end of the day hadn't been enough to spoil it. Yet every time she thought back to it she felt sad that Kezia might still one day mess up Jon's life again. But against that there would be the feelings of a young girl to consider. If Abby wanted to meet the mother that she'd never known, he would not deny her that.

The odds were that Kezia never would come back, so determined had she been, and in the meantime she decided that she, Laura, would do her utmost to fill the gap in Abby's life, if she could. She loved her already. Had done ever since she'd seen her looking after Liam on his first day at school, and she felt the same as Jon, that it was a joy to see them together.

On Monday morning the teacher who'd looked after Liam on his first day at school was waiting to see her. Monica Blake had been diagnosed with diabetes some weeks ago, but at the clinic the week before had been told that her blood glucose was normal. The practice nurse had said that if she stayed on a low-fat diet there was no need to worry about her sugar intake as long as she didn't overdo it, and Monica was confused.

'So, Doctor,' she said, 'I stopped taking sugar in any form and lost a lot of weight that I didn't want to lose, all for nothing.'

'Yes, well, you went off the sugar before the doctors here had a chance to discuss it with you, Monica,' Laura explained. 'And, yes, it did cause weight loss that was worrying at the time. But the thinking about diabetes has changed, and now we tell those who aren't on medication for it that a low-fat diet is the most important thing.'

Monica went away still mystified but delighted to hear that she could indulge a sweet tooth sometimes. Laura's next patient was Ann Stephens, the home help of sheep farmer, Martin Pritchard.

'My hearing isn't good at all these days, Laura,' she said. 'I think I'm going deaf.'

'Maybe you are,' Laura told her. 'But first we'll see if there is any wax in your ears.'

When she'd looked into both of Ann's ears she was smiling. 'You need them to be syringed, but first drop olive oil into your ears for a couple of weeks.'

As Ann thanked her and and got to her feet, Laura said, 'By the way, how is Mr Pritchard getting on?'

Ann smiled. 'We're expecting him home at the weekend and the farmhands and I are going to keep an eye on him.'

'So he's making a good recovery.'

'Yes. He seems to be. Can't wait to get back to the farm, of course.'

'Yes, well, don't let him do too much.'

'We won't. He's a good old guy. We're all fond of Martin.'

It was Wednesday night and Laura was making up the beds in their new accommodation when Jon appeared. He'd told her to take the day off as she'd needed to be at her father's house in the morning when the people hat's very kind of you,' Laura replied, touched by ncern of mother and son. 'Liam will love that, and ld take both children off your hands in the after- s when I finish. But are you sure?'

Yes. I'm sure,' Marjorie told her serenely, with the mory clear of Jon asking, 'Could you cope with ng Liam as well as Abby during the school holidays, m? Laura will still be on the same hours so she'll be e to pick him up at half past three, and Abby won't ed as much to occupy her if she's got Liam around. hey'll keep each other amused.'

'Yes, of course,' she'd agreed. 'Shall I mention it?'

'If you will. I'm trying to avoid Laura thinking that 'm always pulling her strings.'

'I'm sure she doesn't think that,' she'd protested. 'You get on all right living so close, don't you?'

He'd nodded. 'Yes, which is fortunate, as the children are forever wanting to be with each other.'

Life in the apartments was all right, Jon thought that night as he recalled the conversation he'd had with his mother. Soon after she'd moved in Laura had suggested that she make the evening meal for them all, so that he wouldn't have to cook when the late surgery was over. Knowing that it irked her to always be on the receiving end of his thoughtfulness, he'd agreed.

So a routine had established itself with the four of them eating together in her apartment, with the children chattering about their day at school and the two doctors discussing what had been going on down-stairs in the surgery.

from the auction rooms came, and it had given her the chance to move their belongings into the apartment in the afternoon instead of waiting until evening.

Once that had been accomplished she'd taken the keys of the cottage to the landlord and had known that now it was too late to turn back. That she and Liam were about to begin a new phase of their lives and only time would tell if she'd made the right decision.

'So how does it feel, moving on top of the job?' Jon asked as he helped her to ease a quilt into its cover.

'I feel as if Liam and I are like gypsies, never in a settled abode,' she told him.

'Yes, but that's going to change now, isn't it?' There was a hint of anxiety in the question and she knew her reply wouldn't help.

'I hope so. But I've long since learned never to take anything for granted.'

'Am I to take it that there's a message for me in that comment?'

'Only if you want there to be,' she replied, and added to discourage any further questions, 'Where are the children?'

'Watching television at my place and making the most of the novelty of the new arrangements. I came to tell you that I've got coffee percolating and my mother has made a cake in honour of the occasion.'

Suddenly it was all too much and, sitting on the edge of the bed, Laura burst into tears.

'Hey!' he said in surprised concern and, seating himself beside her, Jon put his arms around her for the second time in her life. 'What's wrong?'

'Nothing,' she sobbed. 'You are both so kind. If I don't feel welcome now, I never will, will I?'

'That sounds as if you have doubts about it, Laura. Have you?'

She shook her head. 'I don't know. It's just that I'm used to fending for myself. It feels strange and rather unnerving having my problems solved and being made so welcome.'

'You'll get used to it,' he told her confidently, and, picking up a small lacy handkerchief off the top of a pile that were waiting to be put away, he dried her tears and warned, 'We can't let Liam see you crying. It will spoil the excitement of moving next door to Abby. If you like, I'll go and cut the cake while you powder your nose.' She threw him a watery smile and he went striding off, as if being in her bedroom was nothing unusual.

Later when Abby was asleep and Laura and Liam had gone to spend their first night under the same roof as himself, Jon stood watching the moon over the tops of the peaks and wondered why he had ever thought that taking up where he'd left off with Laura would be easy.

Maybe it was because when they had been young she'd been so uncomplicated and comfortable to be with, but now it was as if she was on her guard all the time, putting up a barrier between them. It hadn't been there on Saturday, when they'd had such a happy day, but it kept appearing and he had the feeling that he was missing something.

He realised that life had been less kind to her than it had to him, and that she wasn't going to be the smiley

Laura of way back any more just to [...] didn't think that was the reason why s[...] on the defensive. There was more to i[...] wasn't going to rest until he knew wha[...]

He was more aware of her with every [...] and amazed at the protectiveness she arou[...] knew he'd treated her badly in the past [...] make up for it, and on that score he was [...] could. But he always sensed withdrawal on [...] when he tried to get closer to her.

She was lovely with Abby and he knew th[...] appalled at the thought of his young motherless[...] mistaking her for the mother she'd never kno[...]

He moved away from watching moonlight [...] moors and went to stand beside his sleeping da[...] His beautiful girl wouldn't miss what she'd neve[...] he thought, and remembering how she'd wanted t[...] close to Laura at the fair his spirits lifted. If there [...] one person beside his mother that he could trust A[...] with, it was her.

It was July. The long summer break from school wa[...] looming and when Laura would have arranged for Liam to be enrolled into the holiday scheme for children with working parents, Marjorie stepped in with a generous offer.

'I have Abby during school holidays,' she told her, 'and as the two of them get on so well, why not let me look after Liam too? It would be no trouble, Laura, and I know that Jon would be happier if your son was with me while you were at the surgery.'

Once they'd cleared away the dishes they separated for the rest of the evening and didn't meet up again, unless one of them invited the other across the landing for a bedtime drink.

That he often lay thinking about Laura as he lay in his solitary bed was something that Jon kept to himself, along with his reluctance to leave her after they'd had that last drink of the day.

He sighed and leaned back in his chair, gazing unseeingly at his computer. He was noticing things about her that had never registered before. The way her eyes sparkled when she was happy. How she bit into her bottom lip with even white teeth when she was undecided about something. But most of all he was aware of how good she was with Abby. If Laura had no tender leanings towards him, it wasn't so with his daughter.

He and Liam were getting on well too. When they were all together the small boy was always by his side, wanting to play football or cricket, and when they went off to the recreation ground and left Abby and Laura doing their thing, he thought that maybe Liam's need for a father figure was as great as Abby's longing for Laura's company.

They were bonding, Liam and himself. So were Abby and Laura. But what of themselves? They were friendly enough down below in the surgery and here up above, but sometimes he saw a look in her eyes that contradicted the smile on her mouth and he wished he knew why. With another heavy sigh, he finished up and went upstairs.

CHAPTER FIVE

As THEY were tidying up after the evening meal on a balmy night in early August, Jon said, 'Do you fancy a stroll by the river before the light goes?' Laura looked at him questioningly and he added, 'There is something I want to discuss with you.'

She was immediately curious about what it could be, but knew one thing that it would not be. Their relationship had settled down into a pleasant sort of camaraderie, with Jon making no demands of her other than in the practice, the children happy in each other's company, and Laura herself taking each day as it came, content to be near him and lost when they disappeared into their separate apartments.

'Yes, all right,' she agreed, and went to tell the children they were going for a walk along the riverbank. They didn't need to be asked twice. To them it was an exciting place with canoeists paddling past and the wildlife that the water attracted along its banks.

As they strolled along, a flock of Canada geese flew in formation overhead, with the setting sun behind them, and Laura thought how wonderful it was to be back in this place that she knew every inch of, with those that she loved so much.

Jon would always have a place in her heart. She couldn't remember a time when she hadn't loved him. Liam was flesh of her flesh, her cherished son, and Abby, the loving, dark-haired child who trusted and loved her in return, was another precious source of joy.

The children were running on in front and as if Jon was tuning into her thoughts he took her hand in his, gave it a squeeze and said, 'Does it remind you of us way back, Laura?'

'Everything reminds me of the old days,' she told him, and was tempted to tell him, *You most of all*, but an elderly man was coming towards them. She'd seen him around the village a few times and remembered him from way back. His name was George Lacey and when he drew level he stopped, ready for a chat.

'Evening to you both,' he said, and with his faded blue gaze on Laura, he added, 'It's Laura Hewitt, isn't it? Welcome back, my dear. You've been gone too long, hasn't she, Jon?'

'I think I can agree with that,' Jon replied, letting her hand go. 'How are you, George? It seems a while since I saw you at the surgery.'

The old man chuckled. 'You're not sorry, are you? I know I'm not. It's because you've been looking after me too well.' He turned to Laura. 'I've never married, but if I'd had a son I would have wanted him to be like this fellow here. And talking of sons, I believe that you've got a young lad of your own.'

'Yes. I have, George,' she told him with a smile. 'He's five years old and his name is Liam.'

'So he'll be the next one climbing over my fence to do some scrumping off my apple trees, will he?' he said good-humouredly. 'Like the two of you used to do.' He pointed to a solid-looking limestone house not a hundred yards away. 'How about calling your young 'uns back and joining me in a glass of home-made elderflower cordial?'

'Yes, why not?' Jon said, and Laura realised that while she'd been gone, Jon and George had formed an affectionate relationship.

As they all sat around a big wooden table with glasses of elderflower cordial in front of them, in the centre of a kitchen cluttered with fishing tackle, George said to Liam, 'Your mother and Abby's dad used to come along here when they were your age. When they weren't at school they used to roam all over the place. I never saw one without the other, and I've a feeling that you children are going to be the same. Am I right, Jon?'

'I think you could be,' he said, smiling across at the children. 'Abby and Liam get on well together, just like Laura and I used to. It's a shame that we all have to grow up.' His glance was on her and Laura saw regret in it and something else that she couldn't quite put a name to.

'We're going to have to make tracks I'm afraid, George,' he said, as if bringing his thoughts back from a far-away place. 'It's school in the morning for our two young ones and bedtime is approaching.'

'Aye, all right,' George said as he got slowly to his feet. 'But do remember that you're welcome any time. It's nice to have some younger blood around the place.'

'He's a great old guy,' Jon said as he waved them goodbye. 'George is content with what he's got and there aren't many of us who can say that.'

'Are you speaking personally?' she asked.

'I might be.'

'Why? You have Abby and your wonderful mother… and the practice.'

'Yes, I know. I'm a lucky man.'

'So?'

I want more, he thought. I want you, Laura. And in that moment all his restlessness and yearnings crystallised. He was in love with her. Totally, committedly, in love for the first time in his life, and with the realisation of it he was speechless.

When he turned to face her she was still waiting for an explanation, and all he could do was shrug and call to the children who were once again way ahead of them to slow down.

He was silent as they walked the rest of the way back to the apartments and when they reached the landing opposite their front doors he said briefly, 'Goodnight, Laura. See you in the morning.'

Which she took to mean they wouldn't be having a last drink of the day together. So what had happened to wipe out the happy atmosphere down by the river and in George's house? she wondered. It couldn't have been anything she'd said as Jon and his old friend had done most of the talking.

With Abby fast asleep, Jon was lying wide awake in bed, thinking that he must have been blind and stupid to have let Laura disappear from his life all that time ago. Yet deep down he knew it wouldn't have made any difference. It had been Kezia he'd wanted. Laura had been like a wistful shadow in the background that he'd wished would go away, and she had.

She'd become the calm, independent woman that she was now at the same time that he'd been facing up to his responsibilities, and he'd fallen in love with her. It wasn't just an attraction that he felt. He was deeply and achingly in love. So much so that she was never out of his mind for a second. The tenderness she aroused in him made his heart melt, and his loins ached for her with a passion that he'd never known the like of before.

So what was he going to do about it? Nothing for the moment, he thought. They were getting on well together, yet was it just because of the children? There were no signs that Laura returned his feelings and having spoilt things once long ago, he wasn't going to risk it again unless he was sure that she loved him in return.

He had learned to be patient, was no longer the impetuous youth he'd been then. So there was no way he was going to go and knock on her door and ask her to marry him at this moment, much as he longed to do so.

Unaware of the tumult of emotion that Jon was coping with, Laura did some ironing, washed her hair and, after watching the late news on television, went to bed. Her last thought before drifting off to sleep was that he'd never told her what it was he'd wanted to discuss.

The next morning Jon was his usual self, with no signs of the withdrawn attitude of the night before. Having decided that she wasn't going to question him about it, Laura greeted him in a similar manner and the day began its course.

It was almost midday. Jon and Tim had set off on their house calls and Laura was about to do the same when a phone call came through from the Bun and Muffin, the café in the main street of the village, a cheerful little place where good food was served. It attracted a lot of the walkers who passed through Heathermere on their way to the peaks and the moors beyond.

The message was that someone had collapsed in the café and would a doctor come quickly? Deciding that it was as quick to walk as to drive there, Laura grabbed her bag and hurried down the street.

When she opened the door the first thing she saw was a middle-aged man on the floor, unconscious and having the convulsions associated with an epileptic seizure. Ellie Thompson, who owned the café, was kneeling beside him while a scattering of customers were standing around, bemused by the drama that had interrupted their morning coffee.

Laura moved swiftly to his side and told the young café owner, 'OK, Ellie, let me have a look at him. Good that you've put something soft under his head. Can you tell me how long he's been unconscious for?'

'By now about ten minutes, I think,' said Ellie, as Laura checked his response, pulse and breathing, and made sure the clothing at his neck was loose.

'OK, that's a long time so could you ring for an ambulance, please, Ellie?' The convulsions had stopped but he hadn't come round. Thankfully he was still breathing. Laura put him carefully onto his side in the recovery position and asked, 'Does anyone know who this man is?'

It seemed not. No one came up with a name, which wasn't all that surprising as he was dressed, like many of his kind, in walking clothes.

When the ambulance had arrived and taken him on board, the atmosphere in the café lightened. Laura reassured Ellie that she had done all the right things by making him comfortable and keeping him safe from injury.

'The hospital will sort him out now,' she told the worried café owner. 'The poor man will wonder where he is when he comes round, but they'll explain what happened and find out if this has happened before, and make appropriate arrangements afterwards. Don't worry, he'll be fine.'

'Thanks, Laura. Can I offer you a coffee and a scone before you dash off?' Ellie asked.

Laura shook her head. 'Don't tempt me, Ellie. I'd love to linger, but I've got some home visits to make and I'm sure that those on my list wouldn't want to think I'd been snacking in here while they were waiting to see me.'

As she walked back to the surgery to get her car, Laura was thinking about what had happened. It was no wonder Ellie had been apprehensive. It could be quite frightening to see someone having a seizure but, in many cases, a person diagnosed with epilepsy would come out of it within a few minutes and be fine. But some cases were more complicated, such as for this man, and an ambulance would be necessary. She hoped Ellie was feeling a bit better now.

* * *

When she arrived back after doing her house calls Tim was there before her and he said, 'Jon has phoned to say that he's finished his calls and is going into town for an hour to do some shopping. I've put the kettle on so shall we have our lunch?'

She nodded and wondered why Jon hadn't mentioned going shopping earlier. But he didn't have to report all his movements to her, did he? She would have been dumbstruck if she'd known he was heading for a jeweller's with her in mind.

He was crazy Jon thought when he came out of the shop. He'd just bought a ring that might never rest on Laura's finger. But the buying of it had made him feel more positive in his mind. More optimistic that on the day when the right moment came along she would be impressed to know just how long the circle of sapphires and diamonds had been waiting for her.

She was up in the apartment, looking for a medical journal that she wanted to refer to, when he came back, and as he paused by her open front door she noticed that he didn't have any carrier bags with him.

'Hi,' he said. 'What's new?'

'Not a lot,' she told him. 'I was called out to the Bun and Muffin just after you'd gone this morning. A man had a seizure.'

'Did he come out of it all right?'

'More or less. The convulsions stopped but he'd been unconscious for more than ten minutes, so we called an ambulance. I've just called the hospital to check up on him and he's doing OK now. Anyway, did you enjoy your shopping trip?'

'Hmm. Yes. I think so.'

His gaze was on her hands and she looked down to see why, but couldn't see any reason for it and said, 'Last night you said you wanted to discuss something with me.'

'Yes, I know I did, but there is no urgency. It can wait. It's almost time for afternoon surgery and the waiting room will be filling up.' And on that reminder they went downstairs to involve themselves with practice matters once more.

When Jon came back upstairs at the end of the day he came into her kitchen where she was putting the finishing touches to the meal, and said, 'I'm thinking of letting Abby have riding lessons and wondered how you would feel about Liam having them, too. It would be my treat, if that's all right with you, and if they take to it maybe they could each have a pony of their own one day,'

He saw her stiffen and when she looked up from what she was doing there was a spot of bright red colour on each cheek and he knew that somehow he'd hit the wrong note.

'It's kind of you to think of him,' she said quietly, 'but, no, Jon. I'm afraid that it isn't all right with me.'

'Why ever not?' he exclaimed. 'Is it because you think he's too young?'

'No.'

'So it's that pride of yours again.'

'Yes. If that's what you want to call it. I have nothing against Liam learning to ride. I know that we both did and loved it. But I don't want him doing it at your expense.'

He was angry now. "What are you on about? I want to pay for Liam's riding lessons because to me he's like a son. The son I might never have. Why are you always so touchy when I try to please you? Am I still not forgiven for what I did all that time ago?'

'Of course it's not that. As far as I'm concerned you didn't "do" anything.'

He was calming down. 'Why are we arguing, Laura? The main thing is whether you would be prepared to allow Liam to have riding lessons.'

'Yes, of course I would.'

'Good. Abby will be delighted when she knows they are both going to learn how to ride. I know someone who has riding stables. They are at the top of Rabbit Lane, and the owner is called Sarah Carpenter. When she first came to Heathermere I was asked to make her welcome by someone that I knew, so I took her to a party and while she was there I introduced her to the man she has married.'

'So it was the riding lessons you wanted to discuss with me last night.'

'Er, not exactly. I had something else in mind.'

'What was it?'

'As our social lives are somewhat restricted, I wonder if we could go out for the evening some time. I could book a table somewhere and my mother would come over to be with the children, if you haven't any objections to that suggestion.'

She felt like weeping. Jon was kind and considerate and she didn't deserve it. He had their welfare at heart all the time, hers and Liam's, and she repaid him by throwing his generosity back in his face, too proud and stubborn for her own good.

'I'd love to go out for the evening,' she said awkwardly. 'I can't remember when last I did anything like that.'

'Good. So how about this coming Saturday when we won't have been on the run at the surgery all day?'

'Yes,' she agreed immediately.

'No need to get dressed up. Just be the Laura that I know for once,' was his parting shot as he went to see what the children were doing.

In other words, he didn't want to be dazzled and swept off his feet, she thought. He just wanted good old Laura across the table from him in some restaurant. As she dished out the meal Laura sensed that there'd been a veiled rebuke in what he'd said, and the pleasure of just the two of them socialising together was draining away.

Clearly Jon wasn't enraptured with the person that she'd become, but what did he expect her to be? The same good-natured innocent who hadn't been able to endure watching him mess up his life with Kezia Carter?

When she looked up he was standing in the kitchen doorway, taking in the food cooling on the plates and the cook staring into space. 'Shall I take it in before it goes cold?' he asked.

'Oh, yes,' she replied absently. 'I'll follow you with the gravy.'

He didn't linger after the meal, which for once had been a subdued affair, with the adults thinking their own thoughts and only the children finding something to chatter about.

When Abby had been tucked up for the night Jon once more found himself trying to sort out his thoughts.

He regretted laying down the law about the dinner date that Laura had agreed to. No wonder she was so often restrained in his presence. He was overpowering and bossy, always said the wrong thing, and it was clear that she didn't like it.

He longed for her to give him a sign that she wasn't totally immune to him, but he could wait. It was still there, the elusive something that she hid behind every time he tried to get close.

In the past he'd taken her for granted, but not any more. He was determined that there were going to be no hitches on Saturday night. He'd requested that she be the Laura he knew, he thought with a grim smile, so if she somersaulted into the restaurant dressed in an old T-shirt and a pair of shorts, chewing on a blade of grass, it would serve him right.

Across the landing Laura's thoughts were running along similar lines.

'Don't get dressed up,' Jon had said. Once she knew where he was taking her, *she* would decide what she was going to wear, and it would not be anything presently in her wardrobe.

The opportunity was too good to miss. It would be the first time they had ever dined out together and she couldn't let it pass without Jon seeing her at her best. She'd appeared out of nowhere looking dowdy, but not any more. The caterpillar was gradually turning into a butterfly. So why not make Saturday night the grand finale of the transformation of Laura Cavendish?

The following day, after Laura had picked the children up from Marjorie's, she took them to the small country station in the centre of the village and they caught one of the frequent local trains into Manchester.

If she was going to look her best on their dinner date, she'd decided that the city was the place to go clothes shopping. Jon knew they were going but did not know the full reason why, and as the children usually went everywhere by car, they enjoyed the novelty of the train journey. While she let her thoughts wander to the occasion that was bringing her into Manchester.

That morning before the first surgery of the day Jon had informed her that he'd booked a table for eight o'clock on Saturday night at a restaurant in the city centre, and it was the mention of that which had given her the idea of shopping there.

When he'd made the announcement she'd thought that he had some nerve, taking her to such a place and telling her in the same breath not to dress up.

'Why isn't Jon coming to Manchester with us?' Liam asked suddenly as the train sped along beside a changing landscape. 'I like it best when he's with us.'

'Abby's daddy is looking after the poorly people who come to the surgery,' Laura told him.

That was one reason why he wasn't with them, and another was that she didn't want him to see what she was going to wear until the night. It would have meant buying something to wear in any case, she told herself. She hadn't bought an evening dress in years, and with it she would need a matching bag and shoes.

When the train arrived at Piccadilly Station she took them down below to board a tram that would take them to the centre of the city and the fashion depart-ments of the stores, and as Abby immediately entered into the spirit of the thing and Liam joined in reluctantly, Laura began the task of finding a dress that would make Jon sit up and take notice as well as being comfortable to wear…

It wasn't easy. There were so many deeply plunging necklines, see-through bodices and intentionally uneven hemlines, that she felt she would never find what she wanted.

Soon Manchester's huge working population would come pouring out of office blocks and shops and fill the buses, trains and trams, and she didn't want the children to be mixed up in the mad scuffle. But this was the only time of day she was free, so now it had to be.

Abby saved the day by pointing to a smart black dress that was sleeveless, with a scooped neckline that wasn't too low and a flared calf-length skirt. It fitted just how she wanted it to, and to go with it Laura bought the white beaded jacket that was displayed with the dress. An evening bag and shoes followed without too much hassle, and after another smooth ride on the tram they caught a train home that wasn't too crowded.

'Don't tell your daddy what I've bought, will you?' she asked Abby. 'It's a surprise.'

'Why?' she wanted to know.

'We're going out for dinner on Saturday night. You and Liam are going to sleep at Grandma's.'

Abby didn't seem to have any problem with that but she said, 'You will tell him that I helped you to choose it, won't you?'

'Yes, of course I will,' she promised, giving her a quick squeeze and thinking that was the end of it Laura reached into her bag and produced some sweets. Liam began to munch away contentedly, but Abby had something else to say.

'Are you and Daddy going to get married, Laura?' she asked.

'Whatever makes you ask that, Abby?' she said, completely taken aback.

'I heard somebody say that you should, and I know that he likes you.'

'Who said it?' she asked, trying to sound casual and not succeeding very well.

'Two ladies who'd been to see Dr Gosforth. As they were going out of the surgery one of them said, "Those two should get married. It would be the sensible thing to do."'

'And how did you know she meant us?'

'Because you and Daddy had just gone out together in front of them.'

'Your daddy and I are just friends, Abby,' Laura told her gently with a sick feeling inside. 'But you know that I love you, don't you? That I would do anything for you. All I want is for you to be happy.'

'Yes, I do, and I love you, Laura, but—'

She was saved any further questioning by Liam butting in unexpectedly with, 'If Jon was my daddy, we could play football all the time.'

At that moment the train pulled into the station. Gathering up her packages, Laura ushered them out on to the platform and hoped that the matter they'd been discussing wouldn't crop up again, especially when Jon was there.

Maybe she should warn him, and *that* was an embarrassing thing to have to do. She felt that she'd handled it badly, should have given Abby a clearer picture of her relationship with her father, but at eight years old she couldn't be expected to understand the complexities of the adult mind.

There was nothing she would love more than that the four of them should spend the rest of their lives as a family, but the voting was three in favour and an abstainer, who if he knew what they'd been discussing might feel that he was being drawn into a net not of his choosing.

When they arrived back at the apartments Jon observed the packages but made no comment. He had a meal almost ready and when the children had washed their hands they all sat down to eat.

Laura's trepidation regarding Abby bringing up the subject of weddings again during the meal was forestalled by another subject, momentarily of greater importance, and once again introduced by her.

'I'm going to have riding lessons,' she told Liam, and as Laura watched his eyes widen she thought that Jon hadn't wasted any time in telling Abby what he had in mind, and now he was looking in her direction with an expression that said the next move was up to her, and she knew that it was.

'Would you like to be able to ride a pony, Liam?' she asked of the small boy she loved so much. 'You and Abby could learn to ride together.'

Before she'd finished speaking he was jumping up and down with excitement and crying, 'Yes, please!'

There was a satisfied smile on Jon's face, and when they were clearing up in the kitchen after the meal he said, 'I'm pleased that Liam is just as keen as Abby about learning to ride. If it's all right with you, I'll have a word with Sarah to find out when we can visit the riding school…and *are* you going to let me foot the bill?'

'No, I'm not,' she said firmly but gently, with a quick sideways glance. 'Even though you are the most generous of men. The cheque for the sale of my cottage in Cornwall is on its way to me, so I can easily afford the lessons.'

'It was just that I thought he would like it if they came from me,' he persisted. 'Liam and I are really getting to know each other. I am loving every moment of it, and so is he, I believe. I know that we've been over all this once, but I don't understand you, Laura. There's something you're not telling me, isn't there?'

'What do you mean?' she asked defensively.

'I don't know, but I'm right, aren't I?'

'If you think so.'

'Oh! For goodness' sake! We're together again after years apart, but sometimes you treat me like a stranger. Have it your own way about the riding lessons. We'll go and sort it out on Sunday morning, if that's all right with you.'

'Yes, that will be fine,' she agreed meekly. 'But don't forget the children are spending Saturday night at your mother's. We'll have to pick them up from there. That is, if you haven't changed your mind about us dining out, as I can tell that you're not pleased with me.'

'Confused would be a better description of my feelings, if it's all the same to you,' he said dryly. 'And no, I have not changed my mind about Saturday. I'm looking forward to it, and hope that you are, too.' He looked at her, deciding to test her to see what her response would be. 'Maybe some time on our own is what we're short of.'

He was to be disappointed. She made no comment, just stared at him with her wide blue gaze and he said wryly, 'We'll understand each other one day, Laura, and when it dawns there'll be flags flying and bells ringing.'

When he looked across there were tears on her lashes and he was appalled to think he had made her weep. He couldn't sleep at nights for thinking of her. Everything she said and did was important to him. He wanted to reach out for her, hold her close and wipe away her tears, but he wasn't going to do any of those things. Too many times he'd done the wrong thing and this might be another.

Back in her apartment, Laura sank down onto one of the kitchen chairs and let the tears flow, until Liam came looking for her and asked anxiously, 'Why are you crying, Mummy?'

She managed a watery smile and wiped her eyes. 'I was just having a sad moment, but I'm all right now,' she told him, holding him close, and on that reassurance he went back to playing with his toys.

There was an urge in her to clear the air between Jon and herself instead of continually offending him with

what he saw as awkwardness and overdone independence. She ached to tell him that she loved him. That
the feelings she'd once had for him had come back a
thousandfold, and her youthful affections had matured
into a deep abiding love.

But what would she do if she saw embarrassment in his
expression? The sort of look that said he didn't want to
offend her, but wished she'd keep her fantasies to herself.

Maybe Saturday night would help her to make a
decision. The way it went could be a guideline as to
whether she could risk making a fool of herself. Of all
things she didn't want Jon to think badly of her, and so
far she'd been doing little to prevent that happening.

CHAPTER SIX

IN THE days that followed there was a virus going around that brought with it a high temperature and a dry hacking cough, yet seemed to clear up reasonably quickly, but the waiting room always seemed to be full.

In the evenings once the meal was over, the two doctors took the children to the recreation ground for an hour before bedtime to give them some fresh air.

That and the non-stop activity during the day at the surgery left little time for any further misunderstandings or heart searchings for either of them. But it didn't prevent their awareness of each other as they played rounders or cricket with Abby and Liam.

Every time she laughingly chased balls that he'd hit for a six Jon knew how much he wanted them to be a family. Not so much because Abby needed a mother and Liam a father, but because he needed a wife. A wife to cherish and adore. Crazy fool that he was, he'd let familiarity blind him to how much he cared for Laura, and not knowing how she felt about him was agony.

What he'd had with Kezia had been just a brief mad attraction. Since then he'd taken out a few women and had been pursued by others. But they'd never been what he'd wanted for himself, or for Abby, and with regard to his precious child, if he asked Laura to marry him, wasn't that what she would think, that it was because he wanted a mother for his daughter?

How was he going to be able to convince her that he wanted her because he loved her? Loved the golden slenderness of her and her stubborn integrity. He longed to make love to her with passion and tenderness, and wake up to find her beside him each morning.

Another ball had come whizzing along, and with his thoughts elsewhere he missed it and it flattened his stumps. 'Out!' the three of them called gleefully and Jon playfully put his head in his hands, sending the children into fits of giggles.

As they walked back to the surgery building there was peace between them, and with the children skipping along in front Jon said casually, 'Are you looking forward to Saturday?'

'Of course I am!' Laura replied, and told him laughingly, 'Be warned. I intend to ignore your instruction not to get dressed up.'

'Ah! So you're going to surprise me!' he exclaimed whimsically. 'No jeans, T-shirt and sucking on a blade of grass.'

'I'm not with you.'

'No, of course you're not. Just a little joke of mine.'

When Laura drew back the curtains early on Saturday morning the sun was already shining out of a clear blue sky and as she stood looking out over the peaks, with the promise of the day ahead, her worries and uncertainties were pushed to the back of her mind. Until she heard Liam coughing, and it was the dry bark that she'd heard so many times over the past week.

When she went into his room she found him hot and feverish and saying he was going to be sick, and as she carried him into the bathroom it seemed that he'd picked up the virus that was going around. Yet she still checked to make sure he hadn't got a rash or that the light wasn't hurting his eyes.

Neither of those symptoms were prevailing, much to her relief. So the virus it had to be, and like others of its kind it would probably clear up in a day or two. But not today, she thought. Jon was going to have to cancel their dinner arrangement. There was no way she was going to leave Liam, even with the excellent Marjorie.

After he'd been sick and she'd tucked him up in bed again while his tummy settled down, Laura padded across the landing, still in the robe she'd thrown on when she'd got out of bed, and knocked on Jon's door.

He was dressed in a similar manner and when he saw her he smiled and said, 'It's eight o'clock tonight we're hitting the town, not eight o'clock this morning, and in any case I don't think your outfit is quite right for the occasion.' But when he saw her expression his smile faded.

'What's wrong?' he asked.

'Liam isn't well. I think he's picked up the virus that's going around. But would you come to have a look at him to make sure that you don't think it's anything worse? Doctors don't always think straight when it's their own child that is the patient.'

'Yes, of course I will,' he said immediately, and went to throw on some clothes before heading into Laura's flat.

'Hey, what's all this?' he said gently as Liam looked up at him with fever-bright eyes. 'My young mate being poorly. Are you sure it's not from the excitement of getting me out at cricket?'

Liam managed a smile but it lacked the brightness of his usual beam and he lay docilely as Jon checked him over.

'Glands up a bit,' he said, 'and there is no doubt about the temperature. Has he been coughing?'

'Yes. The same sort of bark we've been hearing all week,' Laura told him.

'Hmm. I thought as much. It will be the virus. I don't think it's anything more serious than that, Laura. Liam needs something to bring his temperature down and plenty to drink. But I don't have to tell you that, do I? After a day in bed, and with the attention of *two* doctors, we should soon have him back to normal.'

He put his arm around her shoulders and held her close for a second. 'So don't worry. After breakfast I'll phone the restaurant and cancel the meal. There will always be another day for that.'

She nodded and thought wryly of the dress that was hanging in the wardrobe. It wasn't going to see the light of day. Instead their rendezvous had turned out to be an anxious bedside consultation with both of them having just got out of bed, and she wondered if Jon was as disappointed as she was.

But if there was one person who was going to understand her concern it was him. Their children were the most important things in their lives. It would have been just the same if it had been Abby that was unwell.

'Do you want a cuppa?' she asked, and he shook his head.

'No, thanks. I've left Abby asleep. I don't want her to wake up and find me not there. I'll come back later to check on our young patient, and you know where I am if you need me.'

Laura was pale, he thought. Her hair tousled from sleep. The robe she was wearing had seen better days, but to him she was beautiful because he loved her. Whatever she'd been intending dazzling him with that evening, it couldn't possibly make him love her any more.

It was a weekend of disappointments. For Jon and Laura no evening out. For the children no sleeping at Grandma's where Curly, Lambkin and Baa the sheep lived. No visit to the stables to see the ponies, and Liam and Abby were being kept apart to try and avoid her catching the virus.

But in spite of everything it was a time of contentment for their parents. For Jon because for once he felt needed, and for Laura who'd been glad of someone to turn to in her anxiety. It was something she hadn't had in recent years and it took away the feeling of aloneness that had always been there at such times.

By Sunday evening Liam was much better. He and Abby were communicating by notes and the novelty of it was keeping them occupied.

'It doesn't take much to keep them happy, does it?'

Jon said laughingly when he came in to check on the patient. 'In fact, Abby is happier than I've ever seen her since you and Liam have come into her life, and he is always smiling. too.'

He had a smile of his own for her as they left Liam writing another note to Abby and went into the sitting room. 'The four of us fit together like the pieces of a jigsaw, don't we? If Kezia were to show up now, I don't think it would bother Abby one bit. She sees you as her mother in everything but name.'

What was coming next? Laura thought as her heart skipped a beat. Was Jon suggesting that they could soon put that right by changing her name to his? That they should marry for the sake of the children?

She would do a lot for Liam and Abby, move heaven and earth for them if she had to. But she'd already had one experience of giving her heart to Jon and getting no response in return. She couldn't contemplate a marriage under the same circumstances.

Since she'd come back to live in Heathermere he'd shown her consideration and kindness, gone out of his way to help her, but she was the last person he was ever likely to see in a romantic light.

He was watching her, waiting for some kind of response, and when it came it wasn't what he was expecting.

'If you are hinting that we should get together for the children's sake, I'm afraid you will have to forget it,' she said levelly. 'You've already told me what you would want from a marriage. I would want the same if I ever marry again, and it wouldn't be a case of being prepared

to make wedding vows for the sake of convenience.
Why consider settling for second best?'

'I wasn't going to suggest anything of the kind. You
presume too much,' he told her flatly, as it registered that
Laura had just done everything except tell him outright
that she didn't love him. 'Just because I mentioned that
Abby loves you as if you were her mother, it doesn't
mean that I've taken note of what she heard a patient
say about us.'

'So she's told you.'

'And you, too, by the sound of it. What did you say
to her?'

'That I loved her dearly, but that you and I are just
friends.'

'I see.'

'What would you expect me to say?'

'Whatever the truth is, and, Laura, you can rest
assured that I would never want you to be a sacrifice on
my domestic altar.'

He was getting to his feet. 'Maybe tomorrow you'll
be thinking more rationally.' And before she could tell
him she was sorry for jumping to the wrong conclusion,
he went.

When she'd dropped the children off at Marjorie's the
following morning, Laura wasn't looking forward to
facing Jon. She'd spent most of the night fretting about
the mistake she'd made in misreading his mind in such
an embarrassing way.

Every time she thought about the cold-blooded
manner with which she'd brought up the subject of them

marrying she cringed. Yet she'd meant every word she'd said, only to be told that there was nothing further from his mind.

What a mess she'd made of it. If she had any sense, she would give up on Jon. There were plenty of present-able men around who would be less difficult to under-stand than he was.

When he'd knocked on her door that morning to leave Abby with her before going down to the surgery, he'd given her a long thoughtful look, but apart from the bare neccessities had made no other comments, and her spirits had dropped even further.

In the middle of the morning, as if the fates had tuned into her earlier thinking, a 'presentable man' appeared in answer to her summoning the next patient, and when he saw her seated behind the desk he exclaimed, 'Laura Hewitt! I don't believe it. I wasn't expecting you to be Dr Cavendish.'

'Cavendish is my married name, Roger,' she told him with a smile. 'Where have you appeared from? I've been back here for a while but haven't seen you around the village.'

'That's because I've been living in France. My firm is involved in a big engineering project there and I've just popped over to see my mother, and what do I find? That not one but two of the friends of my youth are running the village practice. I tried to get an appoint-ment with Jon but he was fully booked, so the recep-tionist steered me in your direction.'

Roger Jameson was the same age as Jon and herself.

The son of the wealthiest landowner in the village, he'd lived in a manor house in large grounds when they had been young, but had always been eager to make up a threesome if they'd let him, and now here he was. A fair-haired man of average height and build, dressed smartly and lookng the part of the village squire. The role that had once been his father's.

'I'm here about my mother,' he said. 'We lost my dad a couple of years ago and she has gone steadily downhill ever since. It hasn't helped, me working away, but that is going to end shortly and I'll be coming back here to live.

'And in the meantime, while I'm here I would like a visit from the surgery to assess just how bad her rheumatism is, and what can be done about it. Mum can hardly walk and lifting anything is out of the question.

'I asked her if she'd seen Jon and discovered that she hasn't consulted anyone. She's become almost a recluse, living on her own in that big place. A woman from the village comes in twice a week, and one evening an old friend calls round, and that's it.

'Can I make an appointment for her to see one of you? I believe you have another doctor in the practice besides Jon and yourself, but I would prefer Mum to be seen by someone that we both know.'

'Yes, of course,' she agreed. 'I'm sure that Jon would prefer to treat your mother himself as I've only just joined the practice, but if they can't fit you in with him at the desk, I will gladly come out to see her.'

He smiled. 'Thanks, Laura. It's great to meet up again. How has life been treating you?'

She shrugged. 'I'm doing OK, though things haven't been easy. I lost my husband and am bringing up my little boy on my own. I've moved into one of the apartments up above.'

'Really! That's a coincidence. It is what Jon is doing too, isn't it. Bringing up little Abby without a mother. You'll be good company for each other. What is the chance of you joining me for a drink in the pub this evening? It's the night that my mother's friend visits, so she won't be alone.'

She smiled across at him. There were no hidden depths to Roger. 'I'll see what I can do,' she told him, 'but can't promise. I'll ask Jon to keep an eye on Liam for me if he hasn't got anything planned, and hopefully will see you there.'

That evening, after they'd eaten together as usual, but in a subdued atmosphere, Laura said to Jon, 'Would you mind being left in charge of Liam once he's asleep?'

'No, of course not,' he told her. 'Where are you off to?'

'The pub.'

'The pub!' he echoed. 'For what reason?'

'To have a drink with Roger Jameson. I saw him in the surgery this morning and he asked me if I would join him there, for old times' sake.'

'Well! He's quick off the mark! When did he get back from France?'

'I don't know. But Roger is concerned about his mother's general health, her rheumatism in particular, and wants one of us to visit her. I told him that I thought you would prefer to do that and he was going to try to get a quick appointment with you. If he can't I will go to see her.'

'What was wrong with Tim seeing her?' he said abruptly.

'He prefers it to be someone that his mother knows.'

'I suppose that is understandable,' he admitted grudgingly, knowing that the last thing he wanted was for Laura to be socialising in any man's company other than his own.

'So you'll let me out for an hour, will you?'

'I said I would, didn't I, Laura? And please don't make me sound like your jailor.'

'I was only teasing, but it will be nice to talk about old times with Roger.'

They left it at that, but his reluctance for her to resume an acquaintance with an old friend hadn't escaped her, and she thought that if Jon didn't want her, why should he be upset at the thought of her spending a short time with another man? He'd always liked Roger just as much as she had. Next to her, Roger had been his closest friend.

Laura was back by half past nine and when Jon heard her coming up the stairs he breathed a sigh of relief. She had been as good as her word, he thought, but, then, Laura always was.

'You didn't have to rush,' he told her, falsely casual.

'I could have stayed longer, but Roger was all set for going into minute details of his wedding plans to a Frenchwoman who he intends to bring here to live, and as weddings are not my favourite subject at the moment, I promised to hear him out another time. But a word of warning. I think he may be going to ask you to be his best man.'

Jon was smiling his relief. So Roger wasn't out to make a quick comeback with Laura, he was thinking. It had been nothing more than an old acquaintance wanting to rebuild a friendship, but it had been a warning. He was really in love for the first time in his life and was making a hash of it, and while he was dithering around, someone could come along and whisk Laura from right under his nose.

He wasn't behaving in character. He was usually a man of action, but not so in this, and there were good reasons why. Two of them were fast asleep in their beds, and if Laura ever did consider marrying him, there would always be the unanswered question of whether she was doing it for them or him. The same idea had occurred to her, if what she'd said the previous night was correct.

Another reason was her independence. If he put a foot wrong when he tried to tell her he was in love with her, it could all go pear-shaped, and what he felt for her was too precious to risk spoiling.

But one thing he did know as they separated, each to their solitary beds, subject to her agreeing, he was going to rearrange their evening in Manchester for the coming Saturday and speak to Sarah at the stables about their plans for the children's riding lessons.

They'd both been very patient as that had also been postponed while Liam hadn't been well, and he knew that Laura wouldn't want their disappointment to be dragged out.

* * *

Jon went to visit Roger's mother at Mallard Hall, and when he saw her he understood her son's anxiety.

Her movements were slow and painful and she leaned heavily on a stick, but there was nothing wrong with her mental processes. Bright grey eyes in a dried-up face recognised him immediately and she asked without any words of welcome, 'What are *you* doing here, Jon Emmerson?'

'Jon is here because I asked him to come, Mother,' Roger intervened.

'You won't go to see him, so I've brought him to you.'

Narrow shoulders were stiffening and when she'd lowered herself painfully into the depths of an easy chair Avril Jameson said, 'You're wasting your time, Jon. All that ails me is old age and a lack of interest in life in general. You know I lost Alistair, don't you?'

'Yes,' he said gravely. 'I attended your husband when he had the heart attack, if you remember.'

'Of course I remember,' she told him with a trace of hauteur in her voice.

'And so what do you want of me now?'

'I want to check you over if that is all right with you. Your heart, your breathing, your mobility, and the rest. I would also like to do some blood tests.'

'What for?'

'Anaemia, calcium levels, rheumatoid arthritis, and anything else that might be making you feel so low, because there are lots of ways I can make your life easier and more pain-free if you will let me.'

'You want to be feeling better for the wedding, don't you?' Roger coaxed.

'Maybe,' was the unenthusiastic reply. 'Though with all the knocking and banging that's going on upstairs, I can't see much prospect of it.'

'I'm getting married in the village church in a month's time,' Roger told Jon, 'and am having the upstairs of this place made into an apartment for Monique and myself.

'Mum never goes up there any more. She has a bedroom down here with an en suite bathroom, and the arrangement will mean that I can keep an eye on her without crowding her too much.'

When Jon had finished examining Avril he smiled. 'Your heartbeat seems fine, Mrs Jameson. It seems regular enough, and your breathing isn't too bad for someone of your age. Have you ever smoked?' She shook her head. 'I thought not. Your main problem is your lack of mobility and there are a few things we can do about that, such as a special diet for one thing, avoiding all the foods that will aggravate the rheumatism, and providing you with pain-relieving medication.

'Normally I would ask you to come to the surgery for the nurses to take blood for testing, but under the circumstances I'm prepared to do it myself while I'm here, if that is all right with you.'

Avril smiled for the first time since he'd appeared. 'I suppose it will have to be, and what's this I hear about Laura Hewitt being back in the village *and* working at the practice? I haven't heard of her in years.'

Neither had I, he thought and it has been my loss. 'Yes. That is correct,' he said. 'Laura is a widow with a small son and she is back with us once more.'

'Hmm. There have been a few surprises of late and not the least of them my son finding himself a wife. I hope Monique won't be pining for the Seine and the bridges of Paris when she sees our old friend the Goyt.'

There was a mischievous twinkle in her eye that made Jon think that maybe Avril Jameson wasn't as crotchety as she had at first appeared.

When he'd taken the blood and told her that he would be back with the results when he'd received them, Roger walked with him to his car. As Jon was about to drive off, he said, 'I met Laura last night in the pub. Did she tell you?'

'Yes. She asked me to keep an eye on Liam while she was out and when she came back she told me that you're getting married.'

'Hmm. I am. I've had a few relationships in my time, but when I met Monique I knew that this was it.'

I know the feeling Jon thought wryly, but in my case the love of my life has been under my nose for ever and I was too blind to see it.

'So, do you think you could do me the honour of being my best man?' Roger was asking, and Jon had to bring his thoughts back into line.

'I'd be delighted.'

'Great! There'll be an invitation in the post in the next few days for you all—Laura, yourself and the children.'

'Is the subject of weddings still taboo?' Jon asked Laura when he got back to the surgery. 'Or can I tell you that you were right about Roger wanting me to be his best man? He's getting married in a month's time and we're all invited.'

'And did you say you would oblige?'

'Yes, of course. I've always got on well with Roger. He's a decent guy, and concerned about his mother, who is a bit of a tartar these days compared to what she was like when we were kids. But I guess she's in a lot of pain. I took blood for testing while I was there. Has the courier for pathology been yet? I'd like them to go in today's collection if possible.'

'No. He hasn't been yet,' she informed him, not taking him up on his comment about weddings, and not sure if she could face the thought of listening to someone else's wedding vows when she would so love to be making her own to the dark-eyed doctor beside her, who had no idea how much she loved him.

Jon had asked Laura if she wanted him to book the meal again for the coming Saturday and she'd said yes, why not, as if she was easy either way.

Marjorie had confirmed once more that she was free to have the children for the night, and on Sunday morning they would go to the riding stables. So it was all going to plan, but a week late.

Sharon Smith, the hairdresser, had been told after a biopsy that the lump in her breast was benign and her relief was plain to see whenever Laura saw her. She'd made an appointment for Saturday morning with her, and also with the beautician who worked above the salon for a facial and manicure.

She wasn't sure if it was a good idea to present herself to Jon as someone very different from her other role, as his neighbour across the landing who he saw first thing in the morning at her worst, or last thing at night when she was drained after the day's demands of motherhood and health care.

But, she thought wryly, if she was going to take the plunge and bring her feelings out into the open, the least she could do was look her best. He wouldn't want to hear what could turn out to be a hugely embarrassing declaration from a frump seated across the table from him.

At present she couldn't think any further than that. What she was contemplating could spoil what they had. But it would achieve one thing. Make clear to him why she was behaving like she was. Not wanting to take favours from him, guarding her independence, yet eager to be with him. Sometimes happy and carefree, and at others remote and unyielding.

The results from Avril Jameson's blood tests came back on Friday morning and when Jon went up to the hall to give Roger and his mother the pathology report he told them that they indicated rheumatoid arthritis.

'I'm going to put you on anti-inflammatory medication, Mrs Jameson,' he said. 'Or we might try gold penicillinine, which is an antirheumatic drug, and for good measure some not too energetic physiotherapy. But we'll see how the medication works first. I'm not promising a cure, but hopefully there should be an improvement in your quality of life.'

'That's good news, isn't it, Mother?' Roger said with overdone heartiness.

Avril found a smile from somewhere. 'Yes, if it works.

If you can make me supple enough to hold my grand-
children when they come I'll be content,' she told Jon.

From Roger came the protest, 'Steady on, Mother!
Let's get the wedding over first.'

'Not everyone does,' was the reply, and Jon wondered
if that was one for him.

It was usually the mother left holding the baby, but
not in his case, and he thought, as he'd done many times
before, if Abby had been Laura's child she wouldn't
have left her under any circumstances. He'd seen the
way she was with their children and knew she would be
the same with any little ones they might have together.
But in the uncertain situation in which they were living
that seemed a vain hope.

In the days when it had all gone wrong his values had
been all haywire, and he'd only come to his senses
when Kezia had suggested what to him had been un-
thinkable —a termination.

Now, incredibly, circumstances had brought Laura
back into his life. He was seeing clearly which way he
wanted to go, and who with, and if he had to wait for
ever, he wasn't going to mess up their lives again.

She was lovely with the children, and caring and
compassionate with the sick who came through the
surgery doors, but he was never sure what her feelings
for him were. Most of the time they got on well, but
there were occasions when he felt that she was far
removed from him. That whatever he did wouldn't be
right. She never showed any signs of being attracted to
him as he was to her.

CHAPTER SEVEN

THE coming weekend would see the last of the long summer break at the village school. September was upon them and a new term for their young ones. As he drove back to the surgery he was remembering Liam's first day there and Laura's anxiety at his reluctance to be left in the strange new world she had brought him to.

Jon had been happy that he'd been the one she'd turned to, and it had increased his desire to take care of her, independent though she was. What would tomorrow night bring? he wondered. A move forward in their relationship, or a step backward?

The moment Laura had been waiting for had arrived. Jon had taken the children round to his mother's and would be leaving them with the promise that tomorrow they would go to see the ponies.

When they had gone she took the new dress out of the wardrobe and as she slipped it over her head and it shimmered down her body, for once she felt beautiful. Her visit to the hairdresser and the beautician had begun the first part of the transformation, but although Jon had seen the results he'd made no comment and her confidence was flagging.

When he came back from his mother's she was on the landing between their apartments, ready and waiting, and his heartbeat quickened. As he moved slowly up the stairs towards her he thought how beautiful she had made herself for him, and immediately told himself that it might be for her own sake she'd taken so much trouble. Didn't they say that women dressed to please themselves?

Passion was making his loins ache, but he'd learnt a lot about self-control over the years, and there was no way he was going to presume anything that wasn't there.

If Laura would just give him a sign to say that she saw him as someone other than Abby's father and her childhood friend of long ago, he would have something to build on. But so far her recognising him as a man with normal desires and emotions seemed to be a long way off, and until she did he was going to hold back.

'Nice,' he said, keeping his arms tightly by his sides to stop him from reaching out for her and letting all his pent-up feelings take over.

She turned away to hide her disappointment. Why should she expect that the way Jon saw her was ever going to change? she asked herself. Nice, he'd said. Big deal!

As they went out to the car his elegance matched her own. Immaculate in a dark suit and crisp white evening shirt, with expensive cufflinks showing at his wrists and hand-made leather shoes on his feet, his was also a transformation from the man across the landing with stubble on his chin, making breakfast for himself and his daughter.

Tonight he came over as any woman's dream man, yet not hers it would seem. She felt her insides knot at the thought of telling him about her true feelings for him. Did she really want to put herself at any further disadvantage with Jon? she asked herself. Why spoil what they had? Because once it was told nothing would ever be the same again.

She was being given the chance to have him to herself for a little while, away from all their cares and responsibilities, and all at once she calmed down. She would let the evening take care of itself, she decided. If the moment presented itself, she would know and would act accordingly.

As they drove out of the village Jon glanced across at her in the passenger seat. She was gazing tranquilly out of the window and he was relieved to see that his lukewarm comment about her appearance didn't seem to have upset her.

Manchester at night was a mixture of the cosmopolitan and the traditional. The cathedral, floodlit and awesome. The Exchange Theatre, rebuilt after bomb devastation, its interior uniquely eye-catching in unusual marbles.

Dotted around the two famous buildings were bars and restaurants, hotels and fast-food outlets, already thronged with those for who Saturday night in the city was a must.

'I've booked a table here in the restaurant,' Jon said as he drove the car into the parking area of one of the big hotels. 'It's been recommended to me by one of my patients who knows that I rarely dine out in the evening.'

'That makes two of us,' Laura told him with the

assumed tranquility still in place. 'Only for me it is never, rather than rarely.'

'So it's a case of the country bumpkins come to town, then.'

'Mmm. It would seem so. Though I feel more like Cinderella going to the ball.'

'We'd better make sure you don't leave one of your shoes behind, then,' he said whimsically.

A few minutes later they were being shown to a table in an impressive restaurant.

To an onlooker the couple at the table in the corner were a smartly turned-out man and woman spending an amicable evening together as they enjoyed the food and chatted. Only Laura and Jon were aware of the undercurrents below the surface.

What would she say if he asked her to marry him outright? Jon wondered, and found himself answering his own question. It would be a repeat of that other time when Laura had told him in no uncertain terms that if he had a marriage of convenience in mind, he could forget it.

She'd obviously thought that he would be prepared to use her for his own benefit. So to tell her that any thoughts of marriage he'd had were because he wanted her more than anything else in the world would fall flat after that outburst.

Sitting across the table from him, Laura was thinking that it had been a wise decision not to bring her feelings for him out into the open until she was sure that the moment was right. Jon had just raised his glass and said with a twinkly smile, 'To you, Laura, friend, neighbour, colleague.'

He was spelling out the roles she played in his life and all of them were minor compared to the one she wanted to play, and as he looked at her expectantly, waiting for a reply, she said the first thing that came into her head.

'I wonder what the children are doing at this moment.'

'Sleeping, I would hope,' he said, a hint of impatience in his voice. 'It *is* eleven o'clock.'

'It will seem strange when we get back, neither of them being there, won't it?' she went on.

'If you say so,' he replied, and the impatience was still there.

The pleasant atmosphere they'd managed during the meal was disappearing fast. For the first time ever Jon didn't want to talk about the children she thought, not tuning in to his desperation to talk about *themselves* for once.

Shortly afterwards he said, 'Shall we make tracks as you are so concerned about Liam and Abby? But my mother is quite capable of taking care of them, you know.'

'Yes. I do know that,' she told him with heightened colour.

'Hmm. So it was too much to expect that we might have talked about ourselves for once?'

He'd had enough of putting on an act and just wanted it to be over, Jon was thinking. As usual he'd been giving off all the wrong vibes and any hopes he'd had of them becoming closer during the evening had fizzled out.

'You'd already said it all in the toast you proposed,' she told him.

'And what is that supposed to mean?'

'Nothing! Absolutely nothing!'

As he held her jacket for her to slip her arms into, his hand brushed against her neck and he felt her stiffen at the touch, but instead of giving himself time to consider how his touch might have affected her, he said, 'Sorry.' And turned away.

'So what have I done?' Laura asked as they drove out of the city. 'Why did mentioning the children irritate you? Abby is always your first concern, surely.'

'You know she is,' he said abruptly. 'But it isn't to the extent that I care for no one else.'

'Yes. I know that. There is your mother, and you're fond of Liam, for which I'm grateful.'

'Oh, for goodness' sake!' he exclaimed. '*You don't have to be grateful.* He's a smashing kid. But did we really plan this evening with our respective children as the one topic of conversation?'

He'd wanted her to himself for once. Wanted her so badly, he knew if he spoke again he wouldn't be able to stop himself from telling her just how much she meant to him. So he fell silent for the rest of the journey, and, having no ready answer to the question, Laura did likewise.

When they arrived back at the apartments she went straight upstairs without waiting while he parked the car, and went in and shut her door. It had been a disaster, she thought dismally. From a pleasant enough beginning they'd ended up bickering because they'd both got their wires crossed.

She'd taken off the dress and was standing in the satin slip she'd worn beneath it when she heard Jon coming up the stairs. He halted on the landing and she waited

to see what he would do next. She heard his door open
and close and thought that was it. The end of a cata-
strophic evening.

A moment later it opened again and he was knocking
on her door. She didn't move.

'Let me in, Laura,' he called.

Trancelike, she pulled back the catch and with one
stride he was inside and they were almost touching. His
glance was taking in the rise and fall of her breasts
inside the silk slip, the smooth contours of her thighs,
and the uncertainties of the night faded as she felt her
blood warm to the message in his eyes.

'I'm sorry for spoiling your evening,' he said roboti-
cally, as if some unseen force was controlling him. Before
she could reply she was in his arms. He was kissing her
as if it was their last moment on earth, and she was re-
sponding with a passion that had come out of nowhere.
Until sanity fought its way through the heat of it and she
pushed him away. 'I can't!' she gasped. '*We* can't.'

'Why not?' he said softly. 'We're consenting adults.'

'Consenting to what? Lust?'

He became very still. 'Is that how you see it?'

'How else?'

He sighed. 'Oh, Laura! Every time I think I understand you I discover that I don't know you at all.'

As dismay hit her he went, and this time when she
heard his door close she knew it wouldn't be opening
again before morning.

She'd slept at last, after repeatedly going over in her
mind what had been a very strange evening, which in

its last moments had placed her where she'd always wanted to be—in the arms of the man she loved.

But as always there'd been something to spoil it. Passion had flared up between them, urgent and demanding, yet without any words of love or endearment. It had been a moment of sexual chemistry, nothing more, and having made that bleak decision she'd eventually slept.

Too long, it seemed. She opened her eyes to see that it would soon be time to pick the children up from Marjorie's, and there wouldn't be any sleepyheads there with a visit to the stables to look forward to.

As she raised herself up on the pillows the door opened and Jon came in with a breakfast tray. She goggled at him as he placed it on the table beside the bed, and was even more dumbstruck when he pointed to it and said, as if the previous night's happenings had disappeared into the ether, 'My motives are not suspect. I hope you don't mind me letting myself in with the key that you leave with me for emergencies. We have exactly one hour before we go to pick up the children. I thought breakfast in bed might speed things up.' And on that he went. Not with as much purpose as the night before, but he didn't linger.

There were a couple of reasons for that—one the time factor, and the other Laura, heavy-eyed and still in the satin slip, crumpled and creased, yet just as desirable as the night before.

He'd blown it, he'd thought when he'd gone striding back into his own apartment after those incredible moments when she'd been in his arms. The evening had been a hit-and-miss affair, mostly miss, and instead of leaving it at that and trying to make things right the next day, he'd let his feelings get the better of him. He shuddered as he thought that Laura must have felt he'd seen her as available and ready to oblige.

Yet for a few blissful moments she'd responded, and then the Laura that he knew best had asserted herself. Mentioning the word 'lust' when he'd been carried away by his love for her. As dawn had lightened the sky he'd known that the best way to handle it was to go on as they had been before. Not to make an issue of those few crazy moments.

As they walked to Marjorie's house in the mellow September morning the two doctors were silent, each wrapped up in their own thoughts. Laura was wondering how they were ever going to be able to behave naturally after what had happened the night before, and Jon was trying to find the right words to do that very thing, and not succeeding.

Until the children came running out to meet them. The only question in their young minds was how soon were they going to see the ponies, and, as their parents hugged them, it became almost like any other day in their domestic lives.

Almost, but not quite. Barriers had come down the night before, but others had gone up in their place, and Jon thought that treading carefully was going to be the pattern of the days to come.

Jon's friend Sarah who owned the stables was an attractive, capable-looking woman of a similar age to them-

selves, and when he introduced them Laura found
herself meeting the curious glance of dark hazel eyes in
a tanned face.

'I've heard that we have a new doctor in the village.
It's nice to meet you,' she said with a friendly smile.
'Jon tells me that you and he want the children to have
riding lessons.'

'Yes, that is so,' she told her. 'They are both very
excited at the thought, needless to say. Jon and I learned
to ride when we were young, though on my part I haven't
been near a horse in years. Yet the pull is still there.'

'So once your children have had some training you
could all go riding together as a family,' Sarah said, and
Jon winced as he wondered what Laura would say to that.

It had sounded as if he'd been discussing them with
Sarah, which was definitely not the case. His feelings
for Laura would only be brought into the open when *she*
was ready to listen, and the dawning of that day seemed
far off after the previous night's badly handled moment
of passion.

He needn't have worried. If Laura had got the wrong
impression she wasn't showing it. 'Yes, I suppose we
could,' she replied. 'But there's some way to go before
we'd be ready to do that.' He thought if that wasn't a
double-edged remark, he didn't know what was.

As she showed them around the stables Sarah said,
'I've got a couple of New Forest ponies that would be
ideal for these two young ones of yours to learn to ride
on. They're gentle and used to children.'

'That sounds ideal,' Jon said. 'What do you think,
Laura?'

She smiled. 'I agree.' Turning to Sarah she said, 'May we see them?'

The ponies were stabled further along the yard and when Sarah led them out the children's eyes were wide with wonder and Laura and Jon saw immediately that she was right. They looked just right for their requirements.

'Their names are Mischief and Muppet,' Sarah told them. 'Mischief is the bigger of the two so would be more suitable for Abby, and I always use Muppet for the smaller children like Liam.'

As they admired the ponies' shiny golden-brown coats, Jon said, 'If it wasn't for Mischief having a small flash of white on the face it would be difficult to tell them apart.'

Abby was dancing with excitement, while Liam was standing quite still as he took in every detail of the animals in front of them. Laura and Jon smiled at their different ways of showing their delight.

'Once the children have got the hang of it, I think that Jon and I had better sign up for a refresher course,' she told Sarah.

'He doesn't need to,' she was informed. 'Jon hasn't ridden for a few months, but before that he used to take out one of my chestnuts regularly.'

'I see,' Laura said slowly, and felt as if she was on the threshold of his life again. Why had Jon never said that he went riding regularly?

While Jon was in her office, sorting out the details, Sarah glanced down the yard to where Laura was listening to the children's high-pitched chatter.

'You've found her at last, haven't you?' she said gently.

'What do you mean?' he asked warily.

'The woman you've been waiting for.'

He groaned. 'Don't tell me that it is *so* obvious.'

'Only to me, maybe. I can tell from the way you look at her. What's the story, Jon?'

'I've known Laura all my life in one way, and never known her at all in another,' he said flatly. 'And now that I've come to my senses, I don't think she wants me.'

'You're kidding! If at any time over the years you had given a hint that you were ready for the marriage business, women would have been queuing up, including myself, if you hadn't already introduced me to my darling husband. So what's the problem with Laura Cavendish?'

He sighed. 'It's a long story, Sarah. But I'm working on it, and you'll be the first to know if I ever get it right.'

'You will,' she said confidently.

He shrugged. 'I hope so. I really do.'

For the rest of the day the children talked of nothing but the ponies and as they listened to them lovingly, for once Laura and Jon's thoughts were running along the same lines.

The happiness of their two young children came before anything else and their own uncertainties were shelved for a while. Until in the late evening when the children were asleep she knocked on his door and said, 'When Sarah mentioned us being a family, have you discussed us with her? You and she seemed very close.'

'We are only as close as good friends are, Laura,' he said levelly, 'and, no, I haven't discussed us with her.'

It was true. He might have let go a little when he and Sarah had been watching Laura in the yard with the children, but he had said nothing to her before that.

She nodded. 'I just wondered, may I ask another question?'

'Yes. Go on.'

'Why haven't you been riding since I came back on the scene? Is it anything to do with me?'

'Only indirectly. I've had my mind on other things.'

'Such as?'

'Trying to make up for past wrongs.'

She reached out and patted his cheek gently. 'How many times do I have to tell you that you don't owe me anything, Jon? The only person you owe anything to is yourself.' And before he had time to take the moment any further, it was Laura's turn to go into her apartment and close the door.

The children were back at school and it had been arranged that until it was dark in the afternoons with the approach of Christmas, Laura would take them twice weekly for riding lessons after she'd picked them up, and they would have a third lesson on Sunday mornings when Jon could be there.

They needed riding kit and on the following Saturday the four of them caught the train into Manchester to fit Abby and Liam out with the right sort of outfits, and while they were there to shop for clothes for Roger's wedding, which was in two weeks' time.

For Jon there was no problem. The men involved in the ceremony were wearing morning suits and top hats, but it was an opportunity for Laura and the children to dress up, and as Abby and Liam took in all the exciting things that were happening in their lives, Laura was thinking that twice in recent weeks she had come to Manchester to buy smart clothes. She who'd had no inclination to do such a thing for a long time, and on this occasion the shopping party was complete, Jon was with them. When she'd lived in Cornwall she'd bought clothes for the job, but socialising had been a non-starter.

He was watching her expression from a seat opposite her in the carriage, and when their glances held he said with a smile, 'A penny for them.'

She returned the smile. 'I'm thinking in pounds rather than pence.'

'You mean the big shopping spree that is ahead of us? It's great, though, isn't it? There isn't a dull moment these days, with riding lessons and village weddings.'

There was a lift to his voice and she thought that when it was like this, the four of them together, there were no problems. They *were* a family, a happy one, as long as Jon and herself didn't let it throw them off their guard. One day he might bring another woman into their charmed little unit, and what would she do then?

He hadn't given out any signals since the night he'd kissed her, so she'd been right in thinking it had been a brief moment of sexual chemistry that he regretted. Just as she had regrets about the way she'd behaved like a self-righteous prude.

They arrived in the hustle and bustle of the city and as they went down to the tram terminus below the station, holding tightly onto the children, Laura let the day take hold of her and put backward thinking to one side.

The riding outfits were soon sorted as Sarah had told them where to go, and there was no difficulty in finding a pretty dress for Abby in one of the big stores and a neat shirt and tartan trousers with a matching bow-tie for Liam.

The hardest part came last—wedding clothes for herself, with Jon as an interested onlooker. After a few non-starters she found an elegant dress of blue silk that he immediately approved of, and once it was placed in a smart carrier bag she surprised him by saying, 'For the first time in years I'm going to wear a hat. Something big and stylish, so that I don't let the best man down.'

'*You* have never let *me* down in all the time I've known you,' he said with sudden seriousness.

'Don't!' she protested.

'What?'

'Go down that road again. We've been there too often and it does no good.'

His smile was back.

'All right, oh wise one.'

When she posed for him in a hat that was the same colour as the dress, he thought tenderly that the woman in front of him bore no resemblance to the one who had been on the back step of her father's house on the day that he'd returned to the village.

She'd looked drained, drab, too thin. Barely recognisable as the Laura he had once known. And now here she was. At this moment beautiful and confident. So they must be doing something right.

'You'll outshine the bride if we're not careful,' he teased and saw the warm colour rise in her cheeks.

'I wouldn't want to do that,' she told him. 'When are we going to meet her? It seems strange, all this preparation and we haven't yet met.'

'According to Roger, Monique is arriving from Paris tomorrow. She has a small business there and once they're married they will live here part of the time and the rest in France.'

'And how is his mother?'

'Better since I took her in hand, and feeling brighter, though she won't admit it. She's enjoying the excitement of all the changes taking place in their lives but likes to pretend that she isn't.'

'That's good, then,' she said, and watched as Liam took hold of Jon's hand and gazed up at him trustingly.

She turned away. Why couldn't she accept the idea of them marrying for the children's sakes? she thought. Jon had denied that he'd had any such idea in mind when she'd been so hoity-toity about what *she* wanted and what *she* didn't want. But she'd known that he'd been thinking along those lines in spite of him assuring her that he would never want her to be a 'domestic sacrifice'.

Abby had heard a patient say that it would be the sensible thing to do. Maybe the woman had been right, but it was there again. The dread of taking on more than she could cope with if Jon didn't love her as she loved him.

'So are we going to find somewhere to eat now that we've finished shopping?' he asked, and when she turned back to face them Abby had taken hold of his other hand and they were waiting for her to bring her thoughts back from wherever they'd been.

She loved these three more than life itself she thought, and knew that the children returned her love, but what of the man? What were his feelings? How did *he* see her place in his life? She would give anything to know, and on knowing might see the way ahead more clearly. But he'd asked a question and was waiting for an answer.

'Yes, let's find somewhere to eat,' she agreed. 'Where do you suggest?'

She was going to be putting a dampener on the outing if she wasn't careful, and that wouldn't be fair to either Jon or the children.

'And so what was going on back there?' he asked as they queued in a fast-food restaurant. 'Something was on your mind.'

She sighed. It was too much to ask that he might not have noticed her abstraction.

'I was thinking what a happy and secure picture the three of you made,' she told him, without elaborating.

'Good. Because that is how we want our children to feel, isn't it?'

'Yes. It is,' she agreed. With a feeling that she knew what was coming next, she went on, 'But they won't continue to feel like that if *we* don't have the same feelings of contentment, so I'm happy for things to stay as they are.'

It was far from the truth. The day when she would be totally happy would be the one when he told her he loved her, and if it never dawned she would have to make do with what they had. But not as Jon's wife. She'd had lots of practice at being a good mother without being a wife, and it was a painful role to play.

That night after they'd separated Jon kept thinking about the guarded conversation they'd had earlier in the day. Laura had made it clear once more that she hadn't got marriage in mind. It was as if every time he was ready to declare his feelings, she forestalled him.

But the time was fast approaching when he wasn't going to be warned off. The only thing stopping him was a reluctance to do anything that would make the children feel insecure. They were a happy pair and he wanted them to stay that way. Any friction between Laura and himself could make them feel anxious and that just wasn't acceptable.

He was no ditherer, but it was a situation that was making him feel like one. He'd always thought that if and when he really fell in love, completely and irrevocably, he would sweep off her feet the woman he'd given his heart to.

But it wasn't turning out like that. For one thing that very same woman had turned out to be Laura, who he'd taken for granted for as long as he could remember, until she'd come back into his life and made him sit up and take notice, made him take a fresh look at where he was heading. And now he wanted her so much it was like living with a constant ache inside him, and it wasn't the kind of pain he could write out a prescription for.

He knew that his mother guessed what was in his

mind, but Marjorie was a wise woman and she wouldn't pry, knowing that when he was ready he would tell her. So far he hadn't been able to do that, because his heart was filled with wonder as well as uncertainty, and for a little while he wanted to keep that to himself.

It was Sunday morning and they went to the stables for the children's second session with the ponies. Sarah smiled when Jon and Laura presented the two small figures to her, appropriately dressed and raring to go.

When she brought the ponies out of the stable into the yard she told Laura and Jon, 'Just a slow canter around the yard here will be enough for today, but first I'm going to familiarise the children with the tack. They've got to understand what the saddle, bridle and reins are for, and how their hands and legs, along with their voices, will help to control the animal they're riding.

'Instruction in feeding and grooming will also be part of the lessons. They are things that will help to develop a sense of responsibility towards their ponies. So let's begin!'

Together, Jon and Laura watched Abby and Liam learn to ride, for once completely at peace with each other as they delighted in their children's achievements.

CHAPTER EIGHT

THAT was in the morning. In the late afternoon Roger phoned to say that Monique had arrived and that he was inviting a few people over that evening for drinks and an opportunity to meet the woman he was going to marry.

'Needless to say, you two are top of my list,' he told Jon jovially. 'Will your mother keep an eye on the children for a couple of hours for you?'

'Yes, I'm sure she will,' he replied. 'Laura and I will be pleased to come. What time do you want us?'

'Eightish all right?'

'Yes. We'll be there,' he promised, and when Roger had gone off the line he rang his mother to ask if she would come round that evening.

'Yes, of course,' she said, and without her usual reticence, 'It will be nice to have a wedding in the village. Though I can't help wishing that it could be yours. If you don't watch out, I might get to the altar before you.'

'What do you mean?' he asked in amazement and she laughed.

'I'm just teasing. I have a suitor from long ago coming to see me.'

'Who! Anyone I know?'

'No. Alexander and I were engaged once, but he was obsessed with mountaineering so that I hardly ever saw him. In the end I called it off. He was very upset, but I'd met your father by then and knew he was the right one for me.'

'I see,' he said whimsically. 'So your past is catching up with you, just like mine did.'

'Mmm. But not with so many problems attached to it. Which of the two of you is dragging their feet?'

He sighed. 'We both are, but for different reasons.'

'It will sort itself out, Jon. If nothing else, those two beautiful children will bring Laura and you together.'

When she'd rung off, he thought that, much as they adored the children, if anything ever came of his love for Laura, it would be because they couldn't live without each other. No other reason would do.

At that moment she knocked on his door and when he opened it she said, 'You look serious. What's wrong?'

'Nothing,' he said flatly, as he stepped back to let her in. 'I've just been chatting to my mother.'

'You don't usually look like that when you've been talking to Marjorie.'

'Maybe it's because she's just reminded me that she has a life of her own that has been on hold for a long time because of me. She's expecting a visit from an old flame and was teasing me that hers might be the next wedding.'

'So what would be wrong with that?'

'Nothing. Nothing at all. All I care about is her happiness,' he said abruptly. 'But it seems as if everyone around us is getting on with their lives, except us.' He was giving her an opening. Would she take it? No. It seemed not.

'I don't think we're doing too badly,' she said in mild protest to cover a fast-beating heart. 'Our children are happy and contented. We're both living almost on each other's doorsteps and are employed in the practice. The village is beautiful, the people friendly and caring. What more could we ask?' It was her turn to put out a probe, but it was no more successful than his.

'And on top of all that we've been invited up to the hall for drinks this evening to meet Monique,' he said dryly, having been sidetracked once again. 'What more could we ask? I've accepted on behalf of both of us. I hope that's all right with you. Mum says she'll come round to put the children to bed.'

'Yes, it's fine by me,' she said, ignoring the sarcasm. 'Is it formal? Do we have to dress up?'

'I wouldn't think so. But don't be surprised if his mother starts asking questions. Avril still sees herself as lady of the manor, and she remembers you quite clearly from long ago.'

'There is only one thing that would surprise me at this moment,' she told him levelly, 'and it isn't that.' And before he had the chance to take her up on the comment she went back to where she'd come from, leaving him flatter than the pancakes she'd been intending to make if he'd had a spare lemon in his fruit bowl.

When Roger and his fiancée met them in the panelled hall of the manor house Laura saw that the Frenchwoman was small, smartly dressed, and very composed for someone who was meeting her future husband's friends for the first time.

When Roger had introduced them to her he said, 'Jon is to be my best man, Monique. He, Laura and I have been friends since we were small.'

'That is good,' she said with a smile, and would have said more, but someone else had just arrived behind them, and they moved on to where Avril was holding court in the sitting room with relatives and people from the village seated around her.

When she saw Laura she held out a bony hand and exclaimed, 'Laura Hewitt! I thought you would have been to see me before now. Where have you been all these years?'

As if it was a question that they would all have liked to ask, the room became silent as Laura replied, 'Living in Cornwall with my little boy, Mrs Jameson. I came back for my father's funeral and decided to stay.'

She wondered what the interested onlookers would think if she were to say that the reason for her staying was standing right beside her, hiding a smile as his prophesy came to pass.

'Get me away from here,' she said in a low voice, 'before Avril remembers how I once lay on her pale blue chaise longue with my boots on when I had stomach-ache after eating too much fruit off the trees.'

The couple who'd arrived just after them were approaching their hostess and Jon took her arm and guided her behind a big aspidistra in a corner of the room, and as they laughed together he said softly, 'You're lovely when you laugh, Laura. You should do it more often.'

As their glances held he kissed her fleetingly on the lips and it was there again. The raw need that had appeared from nowhere when they'd arrived home on the night they'd dined in Manchester. But if ever there was a time and place that wasn't right, it was while they were skulking behind a potted plant in Avril Jameson's crowded sitting room with the lady herself only feet away.

'Has anyone seen Jon?' Roger was asking, and as they appeared, feigning an interest in the plant, he said, 'How would you be fixed for a rehearsal of the wedding ceremony in the church one evening during the coming week, so that Monique can get the feel of the place? The vicar and his wife are here so I can arrange it with him now.'

'Yes, of course,' he agreed. 'Let me know which night and I'll be there. What about bridesmaids?'

'Monique's sister is coming over with her father, who is going to give her away.'

Laura had turned away. This wedding was going to be a bit too close to home, she was thinking. Fortunately the church would be packed, so maybe it would go unnoticed that the doctor in the blue dress and the big blue hat couldn't take her eyes off the best man.

They gave the vicar and his wife a lift home at the end of the evening, so there was no opportunity for a rekindling of the flame that had burned for so short a time behind the aspidistra, and as Marjorie seemed in no hurry to go when they got back, that state of affairs continued.

By the time his mother was ready for Jon to drive her

home Laura had decided that maybe it was as well that it had been a fleeting thing. Her thoughts were in a big enough jumble without any further complications.

Both children were asleep and he said, 'Will you keep an eye on Abby while I take Mum home? I won't be long and I'll leave my door on the latch.'

'Yes. I won't go to bed until you're back,' she told him, and off they went.

Minutes later Jon rang to say that there was a problem at his mother's and he was going to be delayed. When she asked what was wrong, he said that they'd arrived to find the kitchen floor awash from a burst pipe and it was going to take some time to get it sorted. Did she mind?

'No, of course not,' she replied. 'I won't go to bed until you get back, no matter how long it takes.'

'Thanks, Laura,' he said, and was gone.

She'd been to have a peep at Abby and found her fast asleep, so settled herself on the sofa in her apartment with a magazine and prepared to wait.

After a while she heard a soft footfall on the landing and it seemed that Abby wasn't as deeply in dreamland as she'd thought. She appeared in the doorway with the teddy bear that she slept with in her arms and asked sleepily, 'Where's Daddy, Laura?'

She patted the sofa beside her and as Abby came over and cuddled up close Laura told her, 'He's at Grandma's, sweetheart. She has a water pipe that has burst and he's sorting it out for her.'

'Can I stay here until he gets back?' she asked, and when Laura nodded, and put her arm around her small shoulders, she closed her eyes and went back to sleep with a contented smile on her face.

At that moment Liam appeared, having heard voices. On seeing Abby asleep, he promptly snuggled up on the other side of his mother and followed suit. As Laura looked down at them, so trusting, so precious, she knew that whatever lay ahead she could never do anything that wasn't in their best interests.

After a while her own eyelids began to droop and she succumbed to sleep herself.

It was another day, another dawn, when Jon came back from what should have been a short absence, and when he checked Abby's bed and found it empty he knew where to look.

None of the three of them had moved. Laura and the children were still asleep on the sofa. She still had an arm around each of them, and as he took in the sight he thought it was the loveliest he'd ever seen. All the chaos of the mess that he and his mother had just coped with was as nothing if he could come home to this.

The first thing he'd done when he'd seen the state of his mother's kitchen had been to paddle through the water to turn off the stop tap. Then had followed a phone call to the emergency services employed by the firm she was insured with to get the leak repaired, and while they'd waited for their arrival he'd begun the mopping up process.

His mother had been remarkably calm while it had all been going on, which was always her way of dealing with worrying matters, and hours later when it had been sorted she'd refused his offer to come back to the apartment with him while it all dried out, telling him that she would be fine and that the fan heaters she'd switched on in the kitchen would soon dry everything up and that he ought to be getting back to Laura and the children.

'All right,' he'd agreed, 'but I shall be round first thing in the morning to make sure you are all right.'

She'd smiled and pointed to the breaking dawn. 'It is first thing in the morning now, my dear. Go home to those you love, and Jon, thank you for being your usual caring self. One day Laura will know herself to be a lucky woman.'

He'd sighed. 'I wish I had your confidence, Mother.'

And now he was back, and in front of him was a reminder that it was he who was the lucky one. He hesitated over whether to wake her up so that she could ease herself off the sofa to stretch her cramped limbs without disturbing the children, but couldn't bear to break up the moment and went to make himself a pot of tea and some toast.

He was seated across from them having the first food he'd had in hours when Laura opened her eyes and gazed across at him, startled. Then feeling the weight on her arms, she looked down at the children and began to slide carefully from under them. When she was upright, still in the dress she'd worn for Roger's cocktail party, she flexed her arms slowly and he said softly, 'How did that come about?'

'Abby came looking for you, and wanted to stay with me until you came home, and Liam heard us talking. Need I say more? But tell me, what's the situation at your mother's?'

'It's been a long, wet night,' he told her wryly, noting that she had been quick to change the subject. 'But it's sorted and Mum's place is drying out.'

'Good. Have you got time for a nap?'

He shook his head. 'It isn't worth it. It will soon be time for the surgery and we know what Monday mornings are like, don't we? But Laura, before we go any further, thanks for being there for Abby. I don't know what I would do without you.'

For a moment he thought he saw hurt in her eyes, but her voice was casual enough as she said, 'You would manage, Jon. You did before.'

That was before you came back to turn my world upside down, he wanted to tell her, but didn't, because a small voice was asking from the sofa if it was break-fast time.

While Jon was getting showered and changed after the night's events, Laura gave the children their break-fast and then went to get ready for the day ahead herself, wondering as she did so if he remembered those moments behind Avril's aspidistra.

If he had he wasn't saying anything and she thought that this was how it was going to be. Their physical need of each other flaring up and then dying down because the attraction between them wasn't equal.

But Monday mornings brought with them other matters to see to besides a busy surgery, like sorting out dinner money and making sure that Abby and Liam had got their swimming costumes and towels. It was the morning when their respective classes went to the baths. By the time that was done Jon was ready to go down to the surgery, and she was preparing to walk the children to school. Another day in their lives was underway.

In the middle of the morning Laura found herself facing George Lacey and she observed him in surprise.

'I know what you're thinking,' he said, noting her expression. 'You're wondering why I'm not consulting Jon. I've been holding back from coming and then, when I do make up my mind, he's booked up for the rest of the week.'

'So what's the problem?' she asked with a smile for the kindly old man.

'I'm having trouble swallowing. Can't get the food down. It's as if there's something blocking my throat.'

'Let's have a look then, George,' she said, and seconds later told him, 'I'm going to make an appointment for you to see someone. There is something there. It's difficult to tell how big it is as I can only see so far down your throat. I will tell the hospital it is urgent, and in the meantime keep to nourishing liquids as much as you can. If it gets any worse, get back to us straight away.'

'Don't worry, I will,' he told her. 'I like my food. Eating is one of the few pleasures left for folk of my age.'

When he'd gone she thought that eating might be denied him for quite some time if it was a tumour in his throat. She had a feeling that was what it might be and if it was, some speedy surgery would be required before the passage was blocked completely.

George had been great that night on the riverbank and she'd smiled afterwards at the way he'd remembered Jon and herself scrumping his apples.

He'd looked like a hale and hearty eighty-year-old then, and it had been clear to see that he had been glad of the company.

But today he didn't look anywhere near so well and she knew that Jon would be concerned about him when he knew why he'd come to the surgery. When she'd rung the hospital and asked for an urgent appointment for him, Laura went into Reception to find another patient's records that she was chasing up an appointment for, and found Kelvin from the fish and chip shop coming out from a consultation with Tim.

'Hi, there,' he said. 'I've got a rash on my hands and face. The doc says it's impetigo and very catching, which means I can't work in the shop until it clears up. My wife will have to take my place and Donna has enough on her hands just looking after my mother, and I won't be able to help with that either. I'm going to have to keep away from both of them. Dr Gosforth's given me some antibiotic ointment and says it should clear up in a week or so.'

'So how about a carer for your mother while you have this problem?' she suggested.

'Yeah. Dr Gosforth says he will get onto Social Services to see if they can help.' He gave a rueful smile. 'These are the times when it isn't a bundle of laughs, being in business. But enough of me. What about you, Laura? Are you back with us permanently?'

'I'm not sure,' she amazed herself by saying, and thought suddenly that maybe she would be better away from Jon completely as she'd been before, instead of pining all the time for what wasn't there.

She had her back to the door of his room and hadn't

heard it open until his voice said from behind her, 'So, aren't we frying today, Kelvin?'

''Fraid not,' their schoolfriend of long ago said wryly. 'Laura has the details. I'm off to the chemist.'

Had Jon heard what she'd said about not being sure what her plans were, she wondered wretchedly? He'd gone back in and closed his door without making any comment, so she had no way of telling.

It had been said without thought in a moment of low-spiritedness and now she was regretting it. There was no way she would take Liam away from Abby. The two of them were inseparable.

Behind the closed door Jon was rigid with dismay. Surely Laura wasn't thinking of disappearing again. Why, for heaven's sake? Abby would be heartbroken if she did...so would Liam...and so would he.

The vision of her asleep with the children curled up close came back to taunt him. It had been a moment of pure joy to see them. So why had she told Kelvin that she wasn't sure if she was going to stay? Whatever happened, he wasn't going to let her leave him again. Even if he and Abby had to go and live in Cornwall.

It wasn't as if they had nothing else in common other than the children. They sparked off tenderness and desire in each other, but it was always a fleeting thing.

She broke into his deliberations by coming in to tell him about George, and when she'd explained what the problem was he frowned. Like herself, he sensed something serious and asked if she'd made him an appointment to be seen at the hospital as soon as possible.

'Yes, of course,' she told him, not meeting his glance and went back to her patients.

Laura was on edge as she prepared the evening meal after she'd picked the children up from school. Had Jon heard what she'd said to Kelvin, she wondered, and told herself she would have a better idea when he came up to join her and the children at the end of the day.

When he came upstairs he appeared to be his normal self on the face of it and she gave a sigh of relief, but he didn't come across for his usual bedtime drink later and after waiting for what seemed like an eternity she went to bed with the uneasy feeling that he had heard what she'd said and was keeping silent until he'd decided what to do.

It was the morning of Roger and Monique's wedding, and at the other extreme the day that old George was due to be operated on for cancer of the throat, and as they dressed for the big event it didn't stop Laura and Jon's thoughts going to where he was facing a life-and-death operation.

October had arrived, with cooler mornings and darker evenings. Yet the sun was shining in a bright blue sky as the four of them walked to the old village church.

When Laura had appeared before them in the blue dress and the big hat it had been Abby who'd told her how lovely she looked. Jon had turned away to stop himself from taking her into his arms and kissing away her doubts and uncertainties. He had too many of his own to lay to rest before he felt equipped to do that.

He hadn't said anything about having overheard her talking to Kelvin, and Laura hadn't mentioned it in case she was wrong and it made life even more complicated. On his part he would be keeping a keen lookout for any signs of her making plans to leave.

They were friendly enough in front of the children, but when Liam and Abby weren't there the atmosphere was strained and she wondered how much longer she could bear the uncertainty of not knowing if he'd heard her.

He still wasn't joining her for that last drink of the day which had been one of their most companionable times, but instead of asking him why she kept hoping that there was another reason less upsetting that would soon be revealed.

When they arrived at the church Jon went to sit in a front pew with Roger, and the wedding ring was passed over into his keeping with a nervous smile from the bridegroom.

Laura and the children sat just behind them and as the place filled up with Monique's relatives and almost everyone from the village, she thought that if she didn't belong to Jon she did at least belong to this community, and to think of leaving it again was lunacy.

She had only realised how much she'd missed Heathermere and its charismatic GP when she came back, and no matter what happened in the future between Jon and herself, she was there to stay. What she'd said to Kelvin had been said in a moment of despondency and if she could have taken the words back she would have done.

As she looked around her Laura saw Avril Jameson sitting regally in the front pew dressed in burgundy brocade, and she gave a gracious nod.

The bride was wearing a wedding gown that had a touch of Paris in its style and design, and as Roger turned to watch her walk up the aisle towards him Laura hoped that the petite Frenchwoman would be happy in the Cheshire village that her husband was bringing her to.

As they made their wedding vows before the altar, Laura's glance was fixed on Jon, standing just behind the bridegroom, and she wondered what was in his mind as the ceremony continued in the old church where they'd both been christened.

Would they ever stand in front of the vicar to be bound together in matrimony? she thought achingly, and felt tears prick. As she lifted her hand to brush them away Abby said in a loud whisper, 'Why are you crying, Laura?'

'I'm just happy for Roger and Monique,' she snuffled, praying that Jon hadn't heard what his daughter had said.

It was a vain hope. He turned quickly and on seeing the tears on her lashes groaned inwardly. Were they because Laura was remembering her wedding day to Freddie? he wondered. She only mentioned him rarely but he got the impression that she'd been happy enough with him.

By the time the ceremony was over and the wedding party was posing for photographs outside the church, the tears had gone and Laura was smiling when the photographer shot the four of them together.

It would be something to remember her and Liam by if she decided to go back to where she'd come from, Jon was thinking. But he was not going to let that happen. If she made any moves in that direction Laura was going to have to accept that he and Abby were going with her, whether she wanted them to or not.

Apart from those few melancholy moments in the church it was a happy day for all concerned, with a reception at The Brambles, a hotel on the outskirts of the village, and in the evening further celebrations at the hall, where a buffet had been laid on.

All in all the occasion had been organised in accordance with what the lady of the manor saw as fitting for their status in the village, and Avril had actually been smiling at the assembled company.

At the evening reception there was dancing, led by Roger and Monique, and then the rest of the guests joined them on the dance floor. Laura was smiling at Abby and Liam trying to cope with the intricacies of a wedding waltz when Jon appeared in front of her.

His duties as best man had kept him occupied so far but now he was taking her hand in his, raising her from her seat and saying, 'We've never danced together before, have we, Laura? It will be a first.'

As their steps matched and he held her close, he said, 'So why were you crying? Was it for Freddie?'

'No,' she said in a low voice.

'So why then? Because of us?'

She nodded and he groaned.

'I'm sorry you are upset,' he said regretfully. 'But it is just that every time I think we are making up for all the wasted years, something happens to take the ground from under my feet.

'Apart from that lovely lad of yours over there, trying to steer my daughter around the room, you haven't had much joy in your life over the past few years and I do so want to make up for that, Laura…if only you'll let me. We were great together once, weren't we?'

'Yes, we were, but circumstances…'

He sighed. 'We've been over all that a thousand times. We need to move on and that is what concerns me.'

'How?'

'You doing another disappearing act on me. Is that how you are planning to move on?'

'No, of course not,' she said quickly. 'I've kept wondering if you heard me that day. It was said in a downbeat moment. I have no intention of doing any such thing. For the children's sake, if for no other reason. They are like brother and sister.'

But we aren't like husband and wife, he thought as the moment lost some of its sparkle, but at least they'd cleared the air and he was grateful for that. He'd had enough of long silences and false heartiness in front of the children ever since he'd heard her say she might not be staying. He wanted Laura on any terms other than that, and if this was as far as they were going to progress he would accept it…for now.

CHAPTER NINE

THE children were asleep. Abby was still in the dress she'd worn for the wedding. She hadn't wanted to take it off, and Liam who'd nodded off while he'd been getting undressed, was half in and half out of his pyjamas.

The blue hat and dress had been put away in the wardrobe and Laura was waiting to see if Jon was going to do what he used to do and join her for a bedtime drink.

Leaving the catch off her door she waited, but he didn't appear. She was on the point of going to bed, having decided that she'd read too much into their conversation at the wedding reception, when he tapped on the door and asked in a low voice if she was still up.

He looked tense and said immediately, 'George asked me before he went into hospital if he could name me as next of kin as he has no one. Needless to say, I said yes, and they've just been on to say that he had a cardiac arrest in the middle of the operation. He's seriously ill and could go any time.'

In that moment they weren't doctors first and foremost. The old man was a friend as well as a patient.

'I'm going to have to go to him, Laura, and I hope I

get there in time,' he said sombrely. 'I don't want George to die alone. I wish you could come with me but…'

'I know,' she said softly. 'Someone has to be here for our children, and I am not down as George's next of kin, so it has to be you. Go to him, Jon, and if he is well enough to take it in, tell him I'm thinking about him. He is a lovely old fellow.'

He nodded. 'I'll ring you if there is any news. Bye for now, Laura. Lock up after me.' He gave a wry smile. 'I was all set for joining you for the last cuppa of the day.'

'There will be other times,' she promised as her world righted itself, and off he went into the dark October night.

He came back the following morning when she was giving the children their breakfast and his expression told her that he had no good news about George.

'He's gone, Laura,' he said gravely. 'George passed away an hour ago.'

'I'm so sorry about that,' she said sadly.

'Yes,' he agreed. 'Yet maybe it was meant. The operation, or its aftermath, could have killed him just the same. At least the old guy isn't having to cope with that.'

'Did you manage to speak to him before he died?' she asked.

'We just had a few words before he lost consciousness and you'll never guess what. George has left his house on the riverbank to me.'

'Oh!' she exclaimed. 'How kind of him. He must have cared for you very much.'

'I was stunned when he told me. But at the moment there are more important things to think about. George has made me his executor. I'm going to have to arrange the funeral. He was well liked and half the village will be there, but you and I will be the only official mourners. Maybe Mum will have the children.'

'She'll want to be there herself.'

'So we'll have to arrange it during school hours.'

'That's a better idea, and now let me make you some breakfast.'

'I won't say no to that, and I haven't forgotten that Abby and Liam have a date with Mischief and Muppet this morning.'

'Aren't you ready for some sleep? You've been up all night.'

Jon shook his head. 'No. I'm fine. I wouldn't want to miss a minute of the riding lesson, and afterwards perhaps we could take a walk by George's house as a sort of gesture.'

'Do you remember the night Mr Lacey gave us a glass of his elderflower cordial?' Liam said as the four of them walked in the direction of George's house beside the river that was dancing along its stony bed.

'Will he see us go past?' Abby wanted to know.

'No,' Laura told her gently. 'Mr Lacey was very sick and didn't get better.'

'He's died?' the two of them questioned, round-eyed.

'Yes, I'm afraid so,' Jon told them, and there was silence among the four of them as they walked past the house that now belonged to him.

George's funeral was in the late morning of the fol-lowing Friday, which gave the two doctors time to clear the morning surgery beforehand. Once the waiting room was empty they left Tim to do the house calls while they went to get ready for the funeral and interment in the graveyard adjoining the church.

Jon had been right when he'd said that everyone from the village who could be there would be, and as he and Laura sat in the one funeral car behind the hearse he was acutely aware that they seemed to be thrown together in every way but the one he so desperately wanted.

He kept consoling himself with the thought that she must have some feelings for him or she wouldn't have allowed their present situation to carry on for so long, but he would give anything to know what was really in her mind regarding the two of them.

Maybe he and Abby ought to move into the cottage on the riverbank, instead of selling it. It would separate the children, but only to a minor degree, and it might bring Laura out from behind the barrier that she was so quick to put up whenever he tried to get close to her.

But first they were on their way to say goodbye to George and he had a feeling that wherever he was, he would be smiling down on them. He'd been deeply touched when the old man had left him his house. So had his mother. Laura was keeping *her* feelings to herself. He knew that she was sad that George had died, but guessed she must be wondering where they went from here.

The service in the packed church was short but very moving, and as they all filed out afterwards in the direction of the graveyard Laura was reminded of her father's funeral where she'd been the only mourner, with just a smattering of village folk there. It had been a telling reminder that most people got out of life what they put into it.

She'd never felt so lonely in her life at that time, until across the field that separated her father's house from Marjorie's, had come striding the man she hadn't seen in years, and she'd begun to live again.

George had been laid to rest and a sombre gathering made their way to the village hall where Jon had arranged for light refreshments to be served by a firm of caterers. Gradually most of those who had come to say their goodbyes filtered away. After a while Laura and Jon decided to do the same, leaving the vicar, his wife and a few of the parishioners still on the premises.

When they reached the lychgate Jon said, 'Do you think George would have approved of the arrangements?'

'He would approve of anything that you did,' she told him. 'Do you remember what he said about if he'd had a son?'

'Mmm. That kind of compliment doesn't come one's way every day.'

He was opening the gate for her to go through when the vicar's wife came rushing out of the hall, 'Ah! Thank goodness you doctors are still here!' she cried. 'Katie, the butcher's wife, who is expecting their second child any time, is having fast contractions all of a sudden. She thinks the baby is coming.'

'What? Now?' Jon exclaimed as they turned back.

'My waters broke a few moments ago,' Katie gasped

when they reached her side. 'Then the contractions started and they're coming fast. I'm not going to have time to get to hospital. I wasn't long with our first child.'

Avril hadn't yet left. She was standing nearby, leaning heavily on her stick, and she remarked dryly, 'We've had the wedding and the funeral. We were only short of the christening.'

As Katie cried out at the onset of another contraction Laura was phoning the emergency services for an ambulance. Pointing to a low trestle table nearby, Jon said, 'Can you manage to stretch out on there if I help you? We'll be able to gauge then just how near the birth is.'

'Yes, but hurry,' Katie begged as another contraction gripped her.

They could actually see the baby's head when they'd managed to ease off the maternity trousers Katie was wearing and Laura said, 'OK, Katie. It's all fine. Your child is almost out.'

'I want Jack!' Katie cried. 'I can't have our baby without him being here.'

'I'll go and fetch him,' someone said, and ran to where her husband was behind the counter in the shop, as yet unaware that he was about to become a father for the second time.

'Try not to push until I say so,' Jon advised.

'I need to,' she cried. 'I don't think I can stop myself.'

'Just hold back for a few more seconds and then you can push all you want,' he urged, and into the hush that had suddenly come over everyone he said, 'Now, Katie! Push!'

With a loud agonised cry she obeyed him and as Laura gently guided the baby's head he was out and howling at the indignity of his coming.

At the same moment there was the sound of running feet and Jack appeared, still wearing his striped apron and with a string of sausages dangling from his shaking hand. A cheer went up as he dropped to his knees beside his wife and son.

'What are you going to call him?' someone wanted to know as Jon and Laura dealt with the placenta. Katie looked down in wonder on the red and wrinkled newcomer. 'How about George?' she said. 'If that's all right with you, Jack?'

'Of course it is,' he choked. 'Today of all days, what better name could we choose?' Looking down at the sausages that were gently swinging to and fro he went on, 'Could somebody go to the shop and tell the customer I was serving what's happened to her sausages?'

As a second messenger hurried off, the vicar said reverently, 'The Lord giveth and the Lord taketh away,' and no one present had any disagreement with that.

The ambulance arrived to take Katie, Jack and the baby to the nearest maternity unit, and as Laura held little George in her arms while his mother was taken on board, she was conscious of Jon's dark hazel gaze on her.

What was he thinking? she wondered. It was too much to hope that his thoughts were running along the same lines as hers as she tried to imagine what it would be like if they had a child, born out of love, and a brother or sister for Abby and Liam.

* * *

It had been an unforgettable experience the two of them bringing that small mite into the world, Laura was thinking as they walked home afterwards. It was fortunate it had been an uncomplicated birth as they'd had no medical resources to hand. But at least they'd been there to give on-the-spot assistance.

They were good together in every way but one she told herself. Working harmoniously in the practice. Always on the same wavelength with the children. But when it came to themselves it all became complicated.

In an hour's time she would pick the children up from school and Jon would go back to the practice for the afternoon surgery. As if he was thinking the same thoughts, he said whimsically, 'Would you say that so far this has been a strange day that is now about to revert to normal?'

She smiled. 'Yes, I would.'

'Why is it that we are so good at coping with everyone else's affairs, yet our own never seem to get off the ground?' he questioned as he'd done once before.

'Maybe it's because we are pulling in different directions.'

'And what direction are you going in, Laura?'

'I wish I knew,' she said lightly, as if it was of no consequence. If Jon was in the mood for an in-depth discussion, she wasn't. It would only bring confusion.

It was on the tip of his tongue to bring everything out into the open, but as he'd waited this long he wasn't going to jump in feet first and spoil everything.

So far Jon still hadn't shown up for that last drink of the day. He'd been bogged down with the funeral arrangements and sorting out the old man's affairs, so that it had been late every night when he'd finished what he'd been doing and she'd been asleep.

But now that George had been laid to rest Jon was feeling more relaxed, and that night, as Laura sat at the kitchen table, drinking a solitary hot chocolate, with a thin cotton robe over her nightdress, he tapped on the door.

'At last!' he said as she took another mug out of the cupboard. 'I've been sorting out some more of George's papers, but don't feel that there is quite the same urgency now that the funeral is over.'

He'd changed out of the dark suit he'd worn for the funeral into jeans and a short-sleeved shirt, and she saw that there were dark shadows beneath his eyes. It had been a stressful time for Jon since George's death. He was tired, she thought, unaware that it came from sleepless nights rather than daytime pressures.

As she observed him Laura was filled with tenderness. He was kind and caring to all he met. Not just to his adored daughter and the mother who was always ready to go the extra mile for him, but to patients and friends as well, and she supposed that she came into that last category.

Ever since she'd come back to live in the village he had done everything possible to make her happy, except for the one thing that she longed for. Yet she couldn't blame him for that because he didn't know the problem existed.

He was smiling at her over the rim of the mug he was holding, asking for nothing more than a few restful moments of her company before going to bed. The bed that she would so love to share.

'It has been quite a day, hasn't it?' he said. 'Saying goodbye to the old George and being present at the arrival of the new one. That was some lusty infant who came into the world in such a hurry. It's a satisfying feeling to know that we were there when we were needed, isn't it? Talk about teamwork!' He smiled. 'Because we are a team, aren't we, Laura?'

His tone was easy, casual almost, only he knew how much hung on her answer. If it was negative, as it often was when he tried to get closer to her, he was going to do what had been at the back of his mind ever since he'd discovered that George had left him his house.

He was going to have the place renovated and refurbished and when it was done he and Abby were going to live there. They needed some breathing space, Laura and himself. Time to sort out their priorities. It had been a mistake to suggest her moving into the apartment that was so close to his. For all he knew, she might feel suffocated by him and was putting a brave face on it out of necessity.

Jon was right up to a point, Laura thought, turning away to avoid meeting his glance, and missing the appeal in it that belied his casual tone. They were a team in every way but one, the one that mattered most of all. When she'd held that tiny baby in her arms she'd been more conscious of it than ever.

'Yes. I suppose we are in some ways,' she told him mechanically. 'But then, we always were...*in some ways*.'

So that was it, Jon thought soberly. No assurance that they might have a future together. He would get in touch with his solicitor and start the wheels turning with a view to moving into George's house once it was all signed and sealed.

The children would still be able to spend lots of time together. He would only be a short distance from the surgery. Abby and Liam could have sleepovers at both places and play by the riverbank as much as they liked, as both were capable swimmers.

The only thing missing would be the foursomes that included Laura, but he would just have to cope with that. They had been delightful times but of late the pain factor had outweighed the pleasure.

The following morning Laura sensed withdrawal in him and knew that it had to be from their bedtime conversation, as they'd been at peace with each other before that. Why couldn't she bend a little, she thought after Jon had gone down to start the morning surgery, instead of being so guarded and on edge every time he started to talk about themselves?

She had just arrived home from picking the children up from school when Jack the butcher called with his four-year-old daughter Tamsin, and presented her with a leg of lamb, steaks, free-range eggs and a string of sausages that he assured her laughingly were not the ones from the previous day.

'It's just to show how grateful we are for what you and Jon did for Katie and baby George,' he said. 'They're both doing fine, thanks to you two doctors.

'We'll be having the christening in a few weeks' time and would like you both to be godparents, if you will.'

'We'd love to,' she told him. 'I'm sure that Jon will be as delighted as I am to be asked.'

He nodded. 'Good. We're on our way to see them now and hopefully they should be home tomorrow. Katie will be delighted to hear that you and Jon are going to be godparents.'

When Jon came upstairs at six o'clock the lamb was crisping in the oven, and when he commented on the appetising smell, Laura explained that Jack had been round and they'd been invited to be baby George's godparents.

'And what did you say?' he asked.

'I accepted for us both. I hope that's all right with you.'

His expression brightened. 'Yes, of course it is. I will be delighted to take on that responsibility.' Grateful that Jack's unexpected visit had lightened the atmosphere, Laura went to tell the children about the christening.

November had come and as the days went past, Jon waited to be told that he was the legal owner of George's house. A structural survey had shown that the actual building was sound and in good repair, but the inside was desperately in need of a facelift.

He was hoping that it would be finished in time for Christmas, but had decided that he wasn't going to move out of the apartment until the new year, as it went without saying that the children would want to be together for Christmas. Just how happy he and Laura were going to be at that special time was another matter, and the outlook wasn't good.

They'd been in the habit of discussing most things that affected the four of them in their everyday lives, but on this occasion he was saying nothing regarding what he proposed to do with the property he'd inherited. And Laura hadn't asked.

In the midst of all the uncertainty came the christening on a Sunday morning in early November, and as Laura, in her role of godmother, looked down at the baby in her arms, Jon thought that it was a moment similar to when she'd held George only seconds after his birth, and once again he would dearly like to know what was going through her mind.

Was she thinking that this child was going to be part of a normal family with no undercurrents and past mistakes to haunt his parents? Or was she wishing that she'd been given the chance to have more children? He wished he knew, but the day had yet to dawn when she confided in him.

It seemed that after losing Freddie to the capricious sea Laura hadn't had any other physical relationships over the years. It was as if Liam and the elderly doctor she'd worked with in Cornwall had been the only people who'd mattered.

And here *they* were again, doing the togetherness thing. To the onlooker united in everything they did, but not quite.

On a grey Saturday morning Jon was given the deeds and the keys to the house The waiting was over. He couldn't leave it any longer. He'd kept putting off telling Laura what he was planning to do, hoping that something would occur to make him think again, but it hadn't.

Now she would have to know and he wasn't looking forward to it. But first he wanted to tell Abby about the changes that were about to take place.

He'd taken her with him to the solicitor's and when they came out he took her for a milkshake. As she sat facing him, drinking through a straw, he said gently, 'You know the house by the river that used to belong to Mr Lacey? Well, it is ours now, Abby. What do you think of that?'

Her eyes like saucers, she asked, 'Are we going to live there? By the river?'

'Yes. We are.'

'With Liam and Laura?'

'Well…er…no. It will just be the two of us.'

Her face clouded over. 'Then I don't want to go. I love Liam and Laura.'

'Yes, I know you do, and you'll still see lots of Liam at school, or when you're having your riding lessons, and he can come over to play any time at all.'

'Yes, but Laura won't be there. She's soft and warm when we snuggle up together, and she loves me, too.'

Lucky you, child of mine, he thought wryly, and told her reassuringly, 'You will soon get used to it, Abby. I'm going to go there this afternoon to see what work needs doing. Do you want to come with me?'

There was silence and he decided that he would say no more about it until he'd told Laura. What he was contemplating was a last attempt to make her see how much they needed each other, without him breathing down her neck all the time, and if it didn't work he would have to have a long hard think.

* * *

Laura had been on edge all the time Jon had been at the solicitor's. Expecting what was coming yet hoping she was wrong. She couldn't settle to anything, and as she watched Liam playing contentedly with his toys, she was dreading any upset for him and Abby.

Yet she couldn't blame Jon if he wanted to take advantage of George's generosity. It would be far more pleasant for him and Abby to live by the riverside than be cooped up above the surgery.

When she heard them coming up the stairs she got to her feet ready for what was coming. Abby didn't appear. He'd unlocked their door and she'd gone straight inside, which was unusual, and she asked, 'Is Abby all right?'

'She isn't very happy at the moment.'

'Why is that?'

'I've told her what I think *you* might have already guessed. I'm going to have George's house renovated and she and I are going to live there.'

'It does seem the sensible thing to do,' she said flatly. 'It looks a sturdy property.'

So that was it, was it? Jon thought. A casual acceptance of what she'd just been told. It made him think even more that he was doing the right thing.

Standing just a few feet away, Laura was telling herself that she hadn't been wrong to keep her feelings from Jon. She'd known it would end like this. That he would grow weary of the present situation and want to spread his wings.

Liam had gone to look for Abby. They could hear them talking in low voices across the landing and Jon said, 'It doesn't have to make any difference to the children. They'll still see a lot of each other.'

'Yes. I'm sure they will,' she said in the same flat tone. 'Having seen the bond that has sprung up between them, it is up to us to see that they do.'

'That goes without saying, Laura. I don't need to be reminded,' he said abruptly, and then added in a lighter tone, 'I'm going up there now to have a proper look at the place. I wanted Abby to come with me but she doesn't want to. Hopefully by the time I get back she'll be getting used to the idea. Do you mind if I leave her here with Liam and you?'

'No, of course not,' she said in a tone as abrupt as his had been. 'Nothing has changed as far as *I'm* concerned. But aren't you worried that she's taken it like she has?'

'Yes, of course I am. Her happiness means everything to me. But children adapt. I'm hoping that she'll soon start getting excited about the move.'

He was trying to sound convincing and not succeeding. It was to be hoped he wasn't making them all miserable for nothing. So far Laura had only shown concern for the children since he'd told her his plans. There had been no obvious upset with regard to herself.

Which made him wonder if he wanted to be swanning around that big house on his own in years to come when Abby had fled the nest. It would be as if he'd stepped into George's shoes.

Jon had only been gone a matter of minutes when Liam appeared with his face all crumpled, and Laura's spirits sank even further.

'Why can't we go and live with Jon and Abby in their new house?' he said tearfully.

'There are reasons that you wouldn't understand, Liam,' she said gently, putting her arms around him. 'Abby isn't going to be far away. You'll still be able to see each other.'

She dredged up a smile and coaxed, 'Why not go and ask her if she'd like some milk and biscuits...and a really big hug from Laura.'

Comforted to a minor degree, he did as she'd suggested and disappeared into the other apartment, while Laura went into the kitchen, with the burden of saying the right things to Abby when she appeared lying heavily on her.

When she turned Abby was behind her, framed in the doorway and looking so woebegone that Laura's heart ached for her. She held out her arms and Jon's daughter moved into them like a homing pigeon, then laid her head on her breast and sobbed, 'I want to stay here. Laura. I don't want to live in that horrid house.'

'Don't cry, Abby,' she soothed, stroking her hair gently. 'The house will be lovely when your daddy has finished with it. He is only doing what he thinks is best for you and him. Surely you'd like to live by the river.'

'Yes, I would, but only if you and Liam are there,' she said on another sob.

This was no good, Laura thought angrily. They couldn't keep fobbing the children off with platitudes. It wasn't right, upsetting them like this, even though it might be best for them all in the long term. Somehow she had to console Abby and Liam, and if it had to be at the expense of her own pride, that was the way it was.

'Drink your milk and eat the biscuits,' she said gently, 'and then how about the three of us putting on our warm jackets and going to having a look at this house? There's a place to tie up a skiff or canoes in front of it. And Jon could show you both how to catch some of the fish in the river. People who live beside it have a special piece of paper that says they can fish in it.'

'Really?' Abby said, and Laura was conscious of a lukewarm show of interest.

'So let's go, shall we, before it gets dark,' she suggested.

There had been a lot of heavy rain in recent days and rather than skipping over its stony bed the river was thundering along at a frightening speed.

Their woes forgotten for a while, the children were running along in front of Laura and soon the house came in sight.

Her heartbeat quickened. She didn't know what she was going to say to Jon when they got there, but hopefully when they came face to face the words would come. She longed to tell him that she loved him. That the children weren't the only ones to be devastated by his decision. But what good would that do? It would complicate matters even further.

The children had spotted something in the river. They stopped and went to the water's edge to get a better look. Abby turned and shouted to Laura to come and see. At the same moment she slipped on mud, lost her balance and went head first into the river, hitting her head on a jutting tree trunk as she fell.

When Laura reached the spot seconds later she saw Abby being hurled along in the pounding waters like a rag doll, and thought she would die of horror.

The house was only yards away and Jon's car was there but there was no sign of him. As Liam stood beside her, transfixed, she kicked off her shoes and cried, 'Go and find Jon, Liam. Hurry!' Almost before the words were out she was plunging in after Abby, striking out towards the small figure that was being swept towards a weir just yards ahead.

Abby could be dead already, she thought frantically, from the coldness of the water and the blow to her head, but if she was swept over the weir onto the rocks below that really would be the nightmare of all nightmares.

Where was Jon? They needed him desperately and he wasn't there. Please come, Jon, please, she prayed.

CHAPTER TEN

JON was pottering about in the cellar when he heard Liam screaming his name up above, and as he flung himself up a flight of stone steps he wondered what he was doing there.

'Where are your mummy and Abby?' he asked anxiously at the sight of Liam's distress.

'They're in the river!' he cried. 'Abby fell in and Mummy is trying to stop her from going over the waterfall and being drowned.'

'What?' Jon bellowed in horrified disbelief. Hurtling through the front door, with Liam following as fast as he could, he ran to the bank and saw Abby in her pink coat just a few yards from the weir, with Laura swimming frantically behind her.

As he threw off his jacket, ready to dive in himself, he saw Laura grab hold of Abby and begin to fight her way to the bank against the rushing waters. Then he was running like someone possessed to where she was trying to heave her onto the towpath.

'I've got her,' he cried as he took his daughter's cold hands in his and pulled her to safety, as she coughed and spluttered. Laura nodded and as the waters continued to pound around her she closed her eyes and began to slip backwards, as if she'd reached the limit of her strength.

'No!' he cried. 'Laura, I love you. Come back! Don't leave us!' He turned to a terrified Liam, 'Son, cover Abby with your jacket.' And then he was in the water beside Laura, reaching out until he got a hold on her and then supporting her as he swam with her towards the bank, and once again he found himself helping another of those he loved most in the world to the safety of dry land.

Voices were coming from somewhere and when he looked up he saw that a group of walkers were running towards them, quickly taking in the horror of the scene before them, and he cried hoarsely, 'Please, carry my daughter into the house. There are heaters and towels in there, and if any of you have a mobile, we need an ambulance fast, or they're both going to die of hypothermia.'

'I'll help you get her inside,' the man in charge of the walkers said as he looked down anxiously at Laura lying white and unmoving on the muddy bank.

'I can manage, thanks,' Jon said grimly as he scooped her up in his arms. As he hurried inside to where the women were removing Abby's wet clothes as fast as they could, he saw that two of the men had plugged in the heaters that he'd mentioned and found some clean but faded bath towels to dry Laura and Abby with.

He was quaking with terror inside, knowing that he could yet lose them both, even though they were still breathing. But he daren't give in to it. It was vital that not a moment was lost in bringing up their body heat.

They wrapped Laura and Abby in blankets that

they'd found in an old bedding box and now they were lying beside George's antiquated but surprisingly efficient electric heaters, waiting for the ambulance.

Both Abby and Laura were semi-conscious and Jon thought frantically that the signs of hypothermia were there, and in Abby's case there could be concussion, too from striking her head on something.

If they'd been anywhere else they could have been placed in a warm bath to bring up the body temperature more quickly, but there had been no hot water in the house for weeks and to try boiling kettles would have been futile.

But the women walkers were filling hot-water bottles from the kettle, and now, decked out in an ill-fitting assortment of George's clothes, Jon was doing frequent body temperature checks.

In the middle of it all there was a traumatised small boy clinging to him for comfort. The poor lamb had already lost his father by drowning and must have thought that the same was going to happen to his mother, and it might have done if he hadn't got Laura out of the water in time. As he cradled Liam to him Jon thought he must have been crazy to think he could live apart from Laura and young Liam.

He still didn't know why they'd been there on the riverbank when he'd left the three of them all snug and warm at home, but that didn't matter now. Nothing mattered except that his beloved family were safe, and with regard to that, *where was the ambulance, for goodness' sake*?

At that same second he heard the wail of its siren as

it approached the back of the house from a side road that ran parallel to the river, and as paramedics came hurrying in and quickly took in the seriousness of the situation, within minutes Abby and Laura were being wrapped in space blankets, and being carried into the ambulance.

As Jon took hold of Liam's hand and prepared to follow them, he turned to the walkers, who were gathered around anxiously, and said with a catch in his voice, 'Thank you, all of you, from the bottom of my heart.' Then he lifted Liam into the ambulance, one of the paramedics shut the door after them, and they were off.

'The children!' Laura cried weakly, holding out a cold white hand beseechingly as she began to surface on the short journey to A and E. 'Where are they?'

'They are here, my darling,' Jon said chokingly. 'Abby is just across from you on the other stretcher, and your brave boy is right here beside me waiting to give you a big kiss, aren't you, Liam?'

Liam smiled for the first time since the moment when Abby had gone hurtling into the river, and bent over and pressed his lips against his mother's worried brow.

She touched his cheek gently, and then with returning anxiety asked, 'Jon, what about Abby? Our beautiful Abby. Is she going to be all right?'

He was holding her small hand and as he looked down at his daughter's white face he said sombrely, 'She swallowed some water but hopefully has brought it all up. I also think she might be concussed. She's swollen around the temples, and Liam tells me that she struck her head on a treetrunk as she fell into the water. So that is a worry, too.

'But, Laura, thanks to you, you wonderful woman,

my girl is alive…and so are you. If we'd lost you both, I shudder to think how Liam and I would have faced the years ahead.' He shook his head, his expression distraught. 'I don't know why you were all down by the river when I'd left the three of you safely at home, but I know that somehow I'm to blame and it will haunt me for the rest of my life.'

She shook her head slowly. 'It wasn't your fault. It was my idea that we come to find you. I thought that if Abby and Liam saw the house again they might be less upset, as children don't always take kindly to change, you know.'

There was no time for further discussion on who was to blame for what. They were in the hospital grounds now and as the ambulance pulled up outside A and E Abby opened her eyes and said tearfully, 'My head hurts, Daddy, and I'm cold.'

'You've had a nasty bump,' he told her gently, 'but we are at the hospital now and the doctors here are going to take care of you, Abby. You will soon be warm. That was some very cold water that you fell into.'

The paramedics were wasting no time. As Laura and Abby were lifted out of the ambulance they were placed on trolleys and taken quickly to an empty cubicle in A and E and within seconds a doctor and a nurse appeared.

Abby was given a skull X-ray and to their great relief there was no sign of a haematoma or fracture present. Just a painful swelling and a lot of bruising was the verdict.

Both she and Laura were still wrapped in the space blankets and were looking less pale as their body heat rose, but there was still the anxiety regarding the amount

of water that Abby might have in her lungs, and until
they had a report on that, Jon knew he wasn't going to
relax for a moment. He wasn't surprised when they
were told that she was going to be kept in for observa-
tion for a couple of days.

'And so are you, Mrs Emmerson, until we are satisfied that you are in good health again,' the doctor said,
adding with a sympathetic smile, 'It's the wrong time
of year for open-air swimming.'

Jon wasn't sure if Laura had picked up on the
doctor's mistake. Her glance was on Abby and it was
full of tenderness as she told the man, 'On this occasion
it was very much the *right time*. I am just so grateful that
I was there.' She held Liam close to her. 'We have two
precious children who mean everything to us, don't
they, Jon?'

He nodded. 'Yes, they do indeed. Just as we mean everything to each other,' he said decisively and hoped he
wasn't wrong about that. Soon he would know the answer.
The moment he had Laura to himself he was going to sort
things out once and for all. Today he could have lost her.
It was a horrifying thought and he wondered if she saw
it that way, too. Or if her love was only for the children
and she was happy for him to stay on the sidelines.

Once Abby and Laura had been settled into a small
side room adjoining the children's ward, Jon rang his
mother to tell her what had happened, but there was no
reply. Minutes later she appeared, her face grey with
shock and anxiety and told them, 'Someone came to tell
me what had been happening down by the river and I
got a taxi here as I was in no fit state to drive.'

Some of Marjorie's habitual calm came back when she saw for herself that the two patients were recovering and she said, "I'll take Liam home with me and tuck him up at my house. The poor child looks exhausted.'

'Yes, and I'm hungry, too,' Liam said in mild protest.

'Go with them, Jon,' Laura said. 'You look great in whatever you wear, but that old cardigan of George's and the baggy trousers are not really you. As you can see, Abby is sleeping naturally now that she's warmed up, and I'm not going anywhere. We'll still be here when you get back.'

'All right,' he agreed. 'But I won't be long. I can't bear to let either of you out of my sight.'

When he'd gone Laura lay back against the pillows and wondered if she'd imagined that Jon had called her his 'darling' when she'd been drifting away from the riverbank. She thought she'd heard him cry that he loved her.

Had it been wishful thinking on her part, or maybe just gratitude on his? She wished she knew. She didn't want to be made to feel that she was loved just because she'd saved Abby.

When they'd left the apartment what seemed like an eternity ago she had once again been on the point of telling Jon her true feelings, but always something was there to stop her. This time it had been of terrifying proportions, and whatever had been in his mind of late she could not let him think he was to blame for what had happened.

Jon was back, looking scrubbed and clean and dressed in his own clothes, but with the anxiety still there until he saw that they were both no worse than when he'd left them.

Abby was still asleep and as he came to stand between their two beds Jon said in a low voice, 'I've brought you something.'

'Fruit? Grapes?' she asked, smiling up at him.

'No. But it has got stones in it.'

He took a small box out of his pocket and went down on one knee beside the bed, and as she stared at him with wide eyes, he took a ring out of the box and said, 'Diamonds, with sapphires to match your eyes. Will you marry me, Laura? But before you give me an answer, I want you to know that I'm not asking you because Abby needs a mother and Liam a father, or because it would be more convenient for the domestic side of our lives if we were married.

'I am asking you because I love and adore you, and long to know if there is any chance that you could learn to love me in return.'

The tears had begun to slide down her cheeks as she'd listened to what he was saying and she told him chokingly, 'Oh, Jon! I've waited so long to hear you say that. I can't remember a time when I didn't love you. I thought I heard you say something when I was about to float away in the river, but wasn't sure if it was wishful thinking.'

He was smiling. 'So, having overheard my frantic babblings before I jumped in, are you going to marry me?'

'Yes,' she sobbed. 'I love you so much, Jon.'

He got to his feet. 'So can I put the ring on your finger?'

'Yes, please.'

'And will you and Liam come to live with Abby and me in The Moorings when it has been made habitable?'

The tears had gone. She was alight with happiness as she told him, 'Anywhere you are is where I want to be. I was desolate when you said you were moving out of the apartment, but I couldn't beg as I had no idea that you returned my feelings.'

He sighed. 'It wasn't until you came back that I realised how blind and stupid I'd been to let you move out of my life, and ever since I've come to my senses I've been in agony as I've waited for a sign that you cared. When you went into that raging torrent after Abby I knew that if you were spared I couldn't wait any longer to tell you how much I love you. So, Laura, can we fix a date for the wedding?'

'How about tomorrow,' she said dreamily, and he laughed.

'It's a bit quick. We might have to wait until the day after…and what do you think about the name for the house?'

'Perfect, everything is perfect. Where did you get it from?'

'When I was rummaging about in the cellar I found a faded sign that said "The Moorings" and thought how appropriate it would be with a new skiff or canoes moored at the front.'

He was looking down at the space blanket that she was wrapped in and said whimsically, 'I'm just longing to hold you in my arms. I hope it isn't long before the two of you are free of these things.'

He looked across at his daughter sleeping peacefully

in the next bed. 'Abby will be so miffed that she wasn't awake when I asked you to marry me, but I think she'll perk up when you start discussing bridesmaid's clothes. Liam will be more interested in going with his new dad to buy a boat.'

'It all sounds so wonderful. I can't believe it,' she whispered.

'It is, and it always will be,' he promised, and she knew that she would never be alone again.

The news was out. The village grapevine was buzzing. It was going to be the wedding of all weddings. Laura Cavendish, neé, Hewitt, marrying Jon Emmerson.

It would be standing room only in the church for that one.

Laura and Abby were home from hospital. Abby had recovered well and was showing no reluctance to go near the river again.

'Just keep away from the edge when it has been raining a lot,' Jon had told her. 'I know that you can swim, but it didn't do you any good because you banged your head when you slipped.'

Abby and Liam had heard the news that their parents were getting married with cries of delight, and as the weeks went by and The Moorings was gradually being turned into an attractive riverside property, their excitement mounted.

For Marjorie there would be double joy on the day she watched her son marry Laura. Her daughter and her family were coming over from Australia for the wedding.

* * *

It was a time of blissful contentment for Laura and Jon as the day they had chosen at Easter approached. Joy and laughter had replaced the anxieties and misunderstandings. Every day that dawned was a gift.

They'd spent their first Christmas together for many a long year in the apartments as the house wouldn't be ready to move into until the spring, and on Christmas morning they had watched the children open their presents in the kind of family setting that they'd both wanted so much for them and that had seemed such a long way off when Laura had first come back to Heathermere.

In pale spring sunshine, in a church decked out with Easter lilies, Laura and Jon made their vows in front of a large gathering of well-wishers. An excited young bridesmaid dressed in her favourite pink and a somewhat bewildered small page boy in smart trousers and a velvet jacket had followed the bride down the aisle to where the love of her life stood waiting.

James Penrose had come all the way from Cornwall to give her away and as he stepped back at the altar, and Jon stepped forward to stand beside her, it was there before them. A future of love and happiness to be shared with their children, and any others that might come along out of their love for each other.

A love that had made mistakes, taken wrong turnings, but at last, deep and abiding, had come to fulfilment.

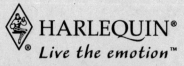

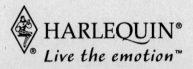

HARLEQUIN®
INTRIGUE®

BREATHTAKING ROMANTIC SUSPENSE

Shared dangers and passions lead to electrifying
romance and heart-stopping suspense!

Every month, you'll meet six new heroes
who are guaranteed to make your spine tingle
and your pulse pound. With them you'll enter
into the exciting world of Harlequin Intrigue—
where your life is on the line
and so is your heart!

THAT'S INTRIGUE—
ROMANTIC SUSPENSE
AT ITS BEST!

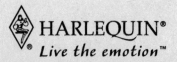

HARLEQUIN®
Live the emotion™

HARLEQUIN®

Super Romance®

...there's more to the story!

Superromance.
A *big* satisfying read about unforgettable
characters. Each month we offer *six* very different
stories that range from family drama to adventure
and mystery, from highly emotional stories to
romantic comedies—and much more! Stories
about people you'll believe in and care about.
Stories too compelling to put down....

Our authors are among today's *best* romance
writers. You'll find familiar names and talented
newcomers. Many of them are award winners—
and you'll see why!

If you want the biggest and best
in romance fiction, you'll get it
from Superromance!

Exciting, Emotional, Unexpected...

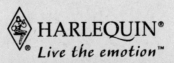

HARLEQUIN®
Live the emotion™

HARLEQUIN® *Presents*

The world's bestselling romance series...
The series that brings you your favorite authors,
month after month:

Helen Bianchin...Emma Darcy
Lynne Graham...Penny Jordan
Miranda Lee...Sandra Marton
Anne Mather...Carole Mortimer
Melanie Milburne...Michelle Reid

and many more talented authors!

Wealthy, powerful, gorgeous men...
Women who have feelings just like your own...
The stories you love, set in exotic, glamorous locations...

HARLEQUIN® *Presents*

Seduction and Passion Guaranteed!

HPDIR08

 **Harlequin® Historical**
Historical Romantic Adventure!

*Imagine a time of chivalrous
knights and unconventional ladies,
roguish rakes and impetuous
heiresses, rugged cowboys
and spirited frontierswomen—
these rich and vivid tales will
capture your imagination!*

*Harlequin Historical . . .
they're too good to miss!*

HHDIR06

Silhouette

SPECIAL EDITION™

Emotional, compelling stories that capture the intensity of living, loving and creating a family in today's world.

Special Edition features bestselling authors such as Susan Mallery, Sherryl Woods, Christine Rimmer, Joan Elliott Pickart— and many more!

For a romantic, complex and emotional read, choose Silhouette Special Edition.

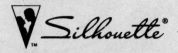
Silhouette®